"I have no right to want you this much."

Emma pushed back and stared up at him, her whiskey-colored eyes bright in the gloom of the cavernous barn. "No right? You have every right, Mac." She reached up and brushed her fingertips along his scarred jaw. "I don't care about this."

He closed his eyes and fought the overwhelming urge to jerk away. To put a stop to the soul-stripping deprivation her assessment generated in his mind.

"It changes nothing. You're honest and good. You protect people…and a horse, and you save lives. You've sacrificed more than the average person ever has and you deserve to be happy."

He opened his eyes, reached up and locked his hand on hers. Staring into her face, he pulled her hand away, severing the intimate touch. He released her fingers, but his push back didn't seem to faze her.

A slow smile bowed her sexy, swollen lips and she stepped back. "I'm fixing supper tonight. I'd like you to come," she said, then left the barn.

He stared after her. How was it Emma always seemed to know what he needed, even if he didn't?

JAN HAMBRIGHT

CHRISTMAS COUNTDOWN

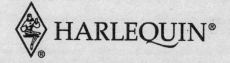

HARLEQUIN®

TORONTO • NEW YORK • LONDON
AMSTERDAM • PARIS • SYDNEY • HAMBURG
STOCKHOLM • ATHENS • TOKYO • MILAN • MADRID
PRAGUE • WARSAW • BUDAPEST • AUCKLAND

I have it on good authority that there are horses in heaven. So, to all of the equines I've had the humble pleasure of saddling up to ride, and brush and love, this one's for each of you: Smokey, Peggy, Whiskey, Moccasin, Brownie, Mid-Bar Dandy, Honey, Starr, Ophelia Mine and Texas.

Recycling programs for this product may not exist in your area.

ISBN-13: 978-0-373-69500-3

CHRISTMAS COUNTDOWN

Copyright © 2010 by M. Jan Hambright

www.eHarlequin.com

Printed in U.S.A.

ABOUT THE AUTHOR

Jan Hambright penned her first novel at seventeen, but claims it was pure rubbish. However, it did open the door on her love for storytelling. Born in Idaho, she resides there with her husband, three of their five children, a three-legged watchdog and a spoiled horse named Texas, who always has time to listen to her next story idea while they gallop along.

A self-described adrenaline junkie, Jan spent ten years as a volunteer EMT in rural Idaho, and jumped out of an airplane at ten thousand feet attached to a man with a parachute, just to celebrate turning forty. Now she hopes to make your adrenaline level rise along with that of her danger-seeking characters. She would like to hear from her readers and hopes you enjoy the story world she has created for you. Jan can be reached at P.O. Box 2537, McCall, Idaho 83638.

Books by Jan Hambright

HARLEQUIN INTRIGUE

CAST OF CHARACTERS

Mac Titus—He's ex-Secret Service, turned bodyguard to a horse? Can he overcome the indignity and the ghosts from his past in time to save the magnificent colt, his determined owner, Emma Clareborn, and eventually the Bluegrass region?

Emma Clareborn—She's got spunk and one shot at pulling Firehill Farm back from the brink of bankruptcy. But putting her trust in the hands of a brooding bodyguard could prove dangerous to her heart.

Navigator's Whim—He's a big bay colt with the speed and training to win the Triple Crown. That is, if his bodyguard, Mac Titus, can keep him safe.

Thadeous Clareborn—He's been raising Thoroughbreds for fifty years and he knows Navigator has "the look of eagles" in his eyes—knowing, confident, fierce.

Sheikh Ahmed Abadar—Absent owner of the horses Victor Dago trains.

Victor Dago—He's the horse trainer for Sheikh Abadar, who Emma has leased her stud barn to, but Victor doesn't seem to know much about horses.

Agent Renn Donahue—Always suspicious, he knows he's on to something big at Firehill Farm.

Sheriff Riley Wilkes—He's one of the good guys who's always looking out for the horsemen of the Bluegrass region.

Rahul, Karif, Omar, Siraj and Javas—Horse trainer Victor Dago's stable crew. But where do their loyalties really lie?

Chapter One

Mac Titus raced for the horse barn with the echo of a woman's scream still reverberating inside his head. He was two hours late, thanks to an accident on the freeway from Louisville.

Was it Emma Clareborn, the woman he'd been hired as a bodyguard to protect? If it was, he'd already blown his assignment.

He ran through the massive doorway into the stable and slid to a stop, prepared for a fight.

The familiar smell of fresh shavings raked his senses, but didn't dull the blade of caution sawing back and forth across his nerves.

All these years he'd wanted to see Firehill Farm again, but not like this. Not with the grip of caution squeezing deep in his chest.

The cavernous stable was dark, the only light emanating from the open door of the tack room in the right-hand corner.

Was she there?

He started to turn for it, but saw a flash of movement to his left.

Pivoting, he saw a man sprint out of the shadows and head for the exit. He was wearing a bandanna to disguise his face and a stocking cap pulled low on his forehead.

Mac bolted and tackled him three feet from the door.

The thug fought hard, rolled over and chucked a handful of sawdust into Mac's face.

Blinded for an instant, Mac snagged the thug around the ankles on the way down and pulled him to the floor.

His captive kicked like a mule, wrenching a single booted foot free from his grasp, and slammed it into Mac's face.

A gash opened. Hot liquid streamed across his cheekbone.

He let go, hoping for another chance to apprehend the thug from a standing position.

Scrambling to his feet, he made another lunge for the bandanna-wearing perpetrator, but the other man beat him by a second, dodged left and ran out the barn door into the night.

Mac shook off the mental annoyance at being a step behind. That's why he was here. That's why he'd been relegated to this detail. To refine his skills again.

Wiping a hand across his face, he cleaned some of the debris out of his eyes and turned back into the barn.

"Miss Clareborn!" He stepped forward, trying to make form out of the shadows. "Emma Clareborn!"

The excited shuffle of horse hooves drew his attention to the first stall where a nervous Thoroughbred paced around inside the twenty-by-twenty-foot square.

He reached his hand through the upper railing to touch the horse's muzzle.

"Get away from him!"

Jerking back he flattened against the wall of the stall, prepared to take on another attack, but the decisive ting of metal boring into wood locked him in place.

"Who are you?" A woman stood in front of him, her eyes wide, her breath coming in gasps that accentuated her state of agitation.

He was glued to the wall where the pitchfork she'd knifed

at him had skewered the folds of his shirt, barely missing the concealed weapon holstered to his belt. He didn't like feeling pinned like a moth to an insect board in science class.

Determination set her features and glimmered in her eyes.

"Mac Titus, your Solberg Agency referral. I'm the bodyguard you hired to protect you from thugs like that."

Her shoulders drooped for a second and she let out a sigh, but the leery stare still haunted her dark eyes. "You have ID?"

"In my wallet."

She didn't move. "Toss it here."

Mac dug into the back pocket of his jeans with his left hand, pulled out his wallet and lobbed it on the ground next to her.

Reaching down, she scooped it up without taking her eyes off of him. Flipping it open, she did a quick comparison. "You look better without blood on your face."

"Are you okay?"

"I'm fine." She closed his wallet and dropped it on the ground. Stepping up, she grasped the handle of the pitchfork in both hands and worked it out of the wall, freeing him.

"It's the second time this week someone has tried to get to my horse. That bandanna-wearing bastard woke me up when he tried to jimmy the latch on the stall door."

Almost on cue the horse in the stable behind him thrust his head over the gate and bobbed his head up and down several times.

"But I'm not your assignment Mr. Titus. Navigator is." She pointed at the horse.

Mac sputtered, dragging the residual particles of sawdust up onto his tongue where he wiped them off with the back of his hand.

"I'm in the business of protecting people, not horses."

"Solberg assured me you could handle this assignment. He claimed you have lots of experience with racehorses."

Navigator bobbed his head again as if he were in some sort of conspiratorial agreement.

Another protest churned inside of him, but he held it in, taking in the subtle shade of sleep deprivation tinting the skin under her expressive eyes, and the cot made up next to the stall gate with a thick sleeping bag to keep out the chill in the December air.

"You've been sleeping out here?"

"Yeah. Every night since I received an anonymous threat over the telephone the day after Navigator won the Clark Handicap at Churchill Downs two weeks ago."

"That's impressive, Miss Clareborn. But he's just a horse, and I usually protect those standing on two legs."

Her eyes went wide, her body stiffened; he'd insulted her.

"He's not just any horse. He's going to win the Kentucky Derby, the Preakness and the Belmont Stakes. The Triple Crown, Mr. Titus."

Navigator bobbed his head.

Amusement glided over Mac's nerves. It wouldn't serve to insult her again, and from the set of her jaw to the surety in her sexy dark eyes, he knew she was certain. He'd seen the obsession before, experienced its destructive power firsthand. People with that much belief in something they couldn't control belonged in Gamblers Anonymous.

"Do you have any idea who's behind the threats against your Thoroughbred?"

"I didn't recognize the voice on the phone and my caller ID registered it as an unknown number. It could be from half the farms in Fayette County, anyone with a Derby prospect. They've been slinking around my practice track, clicking their stopwatches from behind the bushes since early this fall. They've seen the speed he has and they don't want to compete against him."

She stepped to the horse and stroked her hand along the wide white blaze zigzagging down the big bay's forehead.

His head drooped slightly, his eyes blinked shut.

Even a novice could see the woman loved her animal and believed in him, but he knew the inherent error in her thinking.

"I've got a first-aid kit in the tack room. I'll clean you up." She headed for the open door. "Besides I'd like to see what sort of man my money gets me."

Mac scooped up his wallet and fell in behind her as she headed for the tack room in the corner of the barn, watching the sway of her curvy hips clad in tight jeans. The view put an unexpected hustle in his step.

Emma Clareborn was all grown up. A far cry from the girl he remembered seeing once twenty-five years ago. She'd gone from a freckle-faced kid with long, dark braids to a curvaceous woman who at the moment turned up the heat in his blood.

"How long have you been running Firehill Farm?"

"Since my father had a stroke about the time Navigator was foaled."

Mac's footsteps faltered. His dad's old nemesis, Thadeous Clareborn, was still alive?

"It put him in a wheelchair and he never mustered the courage or the physical ability to get out of it." Emma stepped through the tack room door with every nerve in her system attuned to the man behind her. Even bloody and covered with grit he caused an instant attraction just under the surface of her skin.

Dark hair dragged his collar. His five o'clock shadow had advanced well past seven. He was physically just what she'd ordered, but aside from that one question mattered—could he protect her horse?

Mac stepped into the tack room right behind her.

"Sit." She gestured to a stool pushed under the edge of a workbench against the side wall.

Mac pulled it out and sat down, crossing his arms over his chest.

She turned around to reach into an overhead cupboard and grab the first-aid kit. He was unprepared for the sweet smile on her generous lips when she turned back around, or the fact that it was directed at him.

"Solberg did a great job referring you. You're just what I needed—someone who looks the part and fits in with my work crew. No suit-and-tie stuffed shirt, aviator shades…you know, that movie-star-bodyguard type."

"I aim to please." And he planned to give Winslow Solberg a good understanding of the less-than-ideal employment situation he found himself in right now. Bodyguarding a horse. He uncrossed his arms and watched her smile fade.

She cleared her throat and put the kit down on the work counter next to him. "For what it's worth, Mac—I can call you that, can't I?"

Engrossed in the pleasant vibe jolting his body, he almost fell off the stool when she reached out, grasped his chin and forcibly tipped his face up toward the overhead light.

"You can call me anything you like, Miss Clareborn. You're paying the bills."

A slight furrow formed between her eyebrows and smoothed a second later. "Call me Emma, please. Ooh, he kicked you good."

It took every ounce of restraint he had to ignore the heat pulsing from her hand and spreading on his skin. Her grasp was firm, but tender. She let go and opened the kit.

"It's a clean cut. I'll glue it shut."

"Glue?"

"A trick I leaned from my dad. Superglue works wonders on a clean cut. Barely leaves a scar."

Annoyance pitted his thoughts and dragged a reply up his throat, but he clamped down on it. Soon enough she'd discover that scarring was the least of his worries.

Refocusing, he studied her delicate hands as she manipulated a piece of gauze and a bottle of rubbing alcohol.

Curiosity opened up inside of him. He reached out and grabbed her right hand the instant she set the bottle down. Turning it over he stared at the bridge of hardened calluses spanning her palm. "Work crew, huh."

A tinge of color spread on her cheeks. She swallowed hard and pulled her hand back.

"Someone has to make sure Navigator gets his run for the roses."

Irritation flooded his brain, but he didn't have the heart to tell her the odds weren't in her horse's favor. "I'll take up the slack for you, since I'll be here 24/7." He stared into her eyes, but it wasn't appreciation he saw there. "Don't worry. I can protect your horse at the same time."

There it was, a brief veil of relief passing over her features for an instant. He liked it, but it didn't stay long enough.

"I hope so," Emma whispered. She raised the gauze and began dabbing at the cut on Mac's cheekbone. "Things haven't been the same around here since my dad had his stroke." *Not the same* was an understatement, a sweet lie she wasn't proud of, but didn't care to clear up with the muscle-bound protector she'd been forced to hire using some of the farm's draining liquidity. Between her Derby ambitions, Firehill's operating expenses and her father's private nurse, there was no room for financial surprises like having to hire a bodyguard.

Silence encircled them and she focused on her task of scrubbing away the blood and sawdust from the two-inch gash on his handsome face. Her stare locked on his left jawline.

Tension gripped her muscles, forcing her to suddenly withdraw her hand, as if she'd just been scalded.

"One more scar isn't going to make a hell of a lot of difference on me." His matter-of-fact observation was ground out with as much emotion as a traffic cop issuing a citation to an upset motorist.

Sucking in a breath, she continued working, unable to take her gaze off the thick, ruddy scar riding the length of Mac Titus's left jawbone, from his ear to his chin.

She stepped back, watching his dark blue gaze raise to meet hers.

This scar was fresh…this had been a life-threatening injury in his recent past.

"It's none of my business…but how—"

"Did I get it?" He glanced down at the floor, then dragged his gaze back up to hers, and for a moment she thought she saw his rock-hard features soften.

Anticipation bubbled up inside of her and she automatically leaned closer, like a confidante waiting to hear a juicy confession.

The moment burst like a bubble in her face as he stood up.

"The only thing you need to know, Miss Clareborn, is I'm here to make sure nothing happens to your animal. Anything beyond that is off-limits."

She looked at him, measuring the seriousness in his eyes, but there was something else there. Something raw and exposed. Pain?

The shuffle of footsteps rushing into the barn drew her attention to the door.

Victor Dago poked his head into the room.

"My horses are going ballistic, something stirred them up. Everything okay in here?"

Tension snapped in the air. Mac watched hostility spread

across Emma's face, tightening it until he was certain she had some sort of aversion to the man who darkened the doorway.

"Victor Dago, I'd like you to meet my new farmhand, Mac. He took a tumble and spooked Navigator. I'm sorry if it got your horses riled up."

Victor's eyes narrowed. He stepped through the doorway into the room and reached out to grasp Mac's hand. "Nice to meet you. I'm glad to see Miss Clareborn has finally hired someone to help her."

Mac released the man's thick fingers, trying to attach a country of origin to his accent.

"You stable horses here?" he asked.

"Yes, half a dozen, with two still in quarantine via the Virginia Port Authority at Front Royal. They're on day two of a fourteen-day evaluation."

"Anything contagious?"

"No. Just waiting for their Coggins results. They'll come in soon. We'll go to pick them up and put some track time on them before the Christmas Classic at Keeneland on the twenty-fourth."

Emma inched closer to him. If he pushed his elbow away from his body he'd be able to touch her.

"Sorry for the commotion. I'll be more careful next time."

Victor nodded and turned around. "Good night, then." He disappeared through the door.

Emma slumped against the workbench the moment Victor was gone.

Mac sat again, allowing her to finish what she'd started before the interruption. He held comment until he was sure the man had left the stable. "Who is he?"

"He trains horses for a sheikh I've never met or talked to.

They lease my stud barn across the paddock for their racing stables."

The explanation was straightforward, but it didn't explain the visible tension that had sucked the air out of the room less than a moment ago. "I take it you don't like the man."

"He creeps me out. That's all. Close your eyes, this glue is an irritant. It'll burn."

He did as he was told and a few minutes later he was staring at her again, amazed at how little the cut stung, and how beautiful her eyes were.

"Nice fix, doc," he said, patting the closed gash with his fingertips.

She smiled and he resisted the urge to physically smooth away some of the fatigue he could see lining her face. "Why don't you get some rest? I'll take over here. We can talk in the morning."

Emma nodded. For the first time in a month she felt a measure of hope. This battle-scarred bodyguard was here to help, she was sure of it. She stepped out of the tack room and glanced at the blade of light cutting across the barn floor. There, peeking up out of the wood shavings in the exact spot where Mac had tackled the intruder, she saw a syringe.

She reached down to pick it up, but Mac's fingers closed around her wrist.

"Don't touch it. If it belongs to the assailant we might be able to get a print off it."

"It's not mine. I keep my supplies locked up." She straightened.

"Have you got something we can wrap it in?"

"I don't know, I'll look." She moved past him and back into the tack room, where he heard her pulling open one drawer after another.

Mac hesitated and turned his head slightly to the right, listening with his good ear as he stared deep into the darkness, trying to dispel the nagging sensation crawling up from inside his gut. Instinct had saved his hide more than once and now wasn't the time to challenge its validity. They were being watched from somewhere in the wall of shadows built into the nooks and crannies of the barn.

He was sure of it.

Emma shuffled back to his side. "I found a latex glove. Will that do?"

"Yeah." He took it from her and pulled the glove on. Reaching down he picked up the capped syringe by the end of the plunger and raised it to the light coming from the tack room.

"We need to find out what's in this." He studied the syringe full of clear liquid. "It's likely the creep intended to administer it to your horse if he'd gotten into the stall."

Mac carefully pulled the glove off over the syringe, cocooning it in the protective layer. "We have another problem." He turned his attention on Emma.

Her eyes narrowed.

"I think there's someone in the barn. I want you to put this on the bench and come with me."

She didn't protest, didn't question—a good sign, in his opinion. She'd be safer if she followed his lead and let him do the job he'd been hired to do.

Taking the gloved syringe from him, she went into the tack room, put it on the counter and returned to his side as he flipped up the tail of his shirt and unholstered his weapon.

"Stay close."

She nodded and snagged the pitchfork from its spot next to Navigator's stall.

The air thickened around them as Mac focused on the rear exit of the stable. One by one he kicked open the stall gates with his booted foot, clearing the cubicles on both sides of the row as they made their way down the wide aisle.

Staying two steps behind him, Emma wielded her pitchfork like some sort of medieval she-warrior.

He stopped at the last stall door.

The hair on his neck bristled.

Reaching out he shoved it open with his hand and aimed inside, spotting over the barrel of his .44 Magnum.

Empty, save a tabby cat with a mouse in its jaws, who freaked and shot past them, vanishing into the barn somewhere.

"It's clear," he said as he scanned the loft for anything that moved. Nothing. He tried to relax and lowered his weapon. But the sensation of being watched persisted, locking onto his senses with a tight grip that wouldn't release.

Relief softened Emma's features, convincing him to let it go for the night. The search hadn't turned up anyone.

"I'll walk you to the house."

She smiled up at him and turned for the exit. "Thanks. I'll show you the bunkhouse real quick. I stocked the refrigerator, and I'll spot you a couple hours a day so you can clean up."

"Switch to camera one, Agent, and capture a clear shot of his face."

"You've got it." The man flipped a toggle switch on the control panel inside the surveillance van. An image appeared for an instant on the second monitor, then faded to a black screen peppered with white specks. "We've lost camera one again. We'll have to get inside the barn to fix it."

NSA Agent Renn Donahue stared at the blank monitor. "Go back to camera two."

The opposite screen flicked on, displaying a clear image.

Agent Donahue studied the man next to Emma Clareborn as the video streamed in live from the single working surveillance camera hidden high in the stable's hayloft. There was a new player on the scene, but how did he fit into everything?

"Log his image. I want to know who he is and what he's doing at Firehill Farm. He's packing a concealed weapon. Consider him armed and dangerous."

Chapter Two

Mac dumped the last wheelbarrow of manure he'd mucked out of Navigator's stall and pulled off his leather work gloves.

A crisp December dawn was breaking and he watched the first rays of sunlight push through the waves of mist blanketing the rolling Kentucky hills encircling Firehill Farm.

He'd forgotten how much he appreciated this time of morning. The stillness that gripped the air, the cold, quiet peace before another day roared to life and sucked him into its grind.

"Good morning."

The sound of Emma's voice just over his right shoulder jolted anticipation into his blood. He turned around, letting his gaze slide over her curvy body. His impression of her from last night solidified.

She was beautiful, but his eyes had lingered an instant too long, he realized when their gazes locked and he saw color flood her cheeks.

"I see you've done my morning chores." She stepped past him and walked into the barn. "Thank you."

He followed, not totally unaffected by the sway of her hips, or the thick brunette braid brushing the low-rise waistband of her Levi's. Yeah, he liked mornings and this was by far the best one he'd spent in a while.

"My gallop boy will be here at seven to work Navigator."

She emerged from the tack room with a halter, lead rope and a brush. "He needs to be warmed up. We're going for a timed gallop this morning."

Ahead of her he reached out, unlatched the stall door and pulled it open. She stepped past him into the cubicle, dropped the horse brush and put the halter on Navigator.

A nicker rumbled deep in the big bay's throat. He nudged Emma affectionately as she bent over and picked up the brush.

Mac watched her take quick, even strokes across the colt's back and down his withers.

"What's his Beyer Speed Figure?"

She gave him a glance over her left shoulder and continued to groom the horse. "You do know something about racing."

"Yeah." A measure of hesitation pulled back any need he felt to enlighten her about his past in the world of Thoroughbred horse racing, or his knowledge of the Beyer system of combining a horse's race time and the inherent speed of the track into a single performance number.

"It's 126."

A low whistle hissed between his lips. He eyed the bay, pausing on his definable attributes: a well-chiseled head, long neck, deep chest, long legs and powerful hindquarters.

"That's not too shabby. Where'd he last run?"

"Churchill Downs, the Clark Handicap. He won his one and one-eighth mile race by five lengths."

A charge buzzed through him, its pulse almost pushing him over the edge into excitement, but he cut the current off with memories of the disappointment that came after the high. A nose-first dive into reality. One he'd seen many men take. The one that ultimately had claimed his horse-trainer father.

"He's got good confirmation and a great Beyer. He has a

shot." Mac stepped through the stall gate and leaned against the outside wall, his back to her and the horse.

"His great-grandfather won the Derby in 1987."

Mac ran the date in his head, trying to reconcile the edge of anger creeping through his body like poison. He turned back around, clutching the iron bars that surrounded the stall. "Alysheba?"

"Yeah. He sired Smooth Sailing, who sired Nautical Mile, who sired Navigator's Whim."

The world was shrinking and he found himself smack in the middle of it. Smooth Sailing was the horse Thadeous Clareborn had stolen from his father in a claiming race. Now he was the grandfather of a Derby prospect? If the Beyer Speed Figure was any indicator, Navigator's Whim stood a better-than-average chance of winning the Kentucky Derby, and reaching for the Triple Crown.

EMMA PUT HER FOOT INTO the stirrup, grabbed the saddle horn and climbed aboard her pony horse, Oliver. She reached down for the lead rope attached to the colt and Mac put it in her hand. He stepped back, catching her eye from under the brim of a well-worn hat he'd found in the tack room.

His gaze was electric, its intensity arcing through her body with a conductivity that left her breathless.

"It's only forty-four degrees this morning, Emma. Warm him up good."

She nodded. "I'll jog him out a half-mile and back, then meet you at the gate." Reining for the opening onto the race-track, she hoped like crazy he hadn't seen the blush she could feel stinging her cheeks even as the morning mist cooled her skin. She was feeling shy. She'd had a boyfriend or two, but there was something magnetic about Mac Titus, something primal, untamed, sexy and…haunting about the way he looked at her.

Tugging on Navigator's lead rope, she threaded them through the opening and out onto the track.

Layers of fog obscured the mile-and-a-half oblong, but she could see it with her eyes closed; she'd ridden it a thousand times. Even in the dark.

Nudging Oliver into a gentle lope, she focused on the rail at the first turn and relaxed into the saddle.

Mac watched horses and rider fade into the flat gray mist and put his senses on alert. Turning his head slightly to the right, he picked up the whisper of hoofbeats churning soft soil.

He closed his eyes, letting the sight deprivation intensify his auditory ability. He didn't know why it worked, but it did. Closing off one always heightened the other. Up until he'd been shot in the line of duty, he'd never really appreciated his razor-sharp senses or the capabilities they afforded him.

The hearing in his left ear would never—

Mac jerked around at the pressure of a hand on his shoulder.

Caught in an instinctive reaction, he leveled the man with his forearm and shoved him back into the fence rail.

"Easy!" The kid's eyes went wide. He raised his gloved hands in surrender.

The adrenaline in Mac's system diluted as he sized up the young man clad in a coat, breeches, boots and a riding helmet, its loose strap swinging back and forth from the force he'd exerted against him.

"Oh hell, I'm sorry. I didn't hear you coming until you were on me." He lowered his arm and took a step back. "I overreacted. I'm Emma's new groom, Mac. Are you Navigator's gallop boy?"

"Yeah. Josh Duncan." He smoothed the front of his jacket. "I'm early. My 5:30 a.m. ride over at McCluskies' canceled. I came straight here."

"Is Chester McCluskie still running Rambling Farm?"

"Yeah. He has a heck of a Derby prospect himself…had a prospect, I should say, until this morning. His filly Ophelia Mine went AWOL sometime last night, and went down in her stall. Hurt herself pretty bad. They've got the vet there now."

Caution sluiced in Mac's veins. Was it possible Navigator hadn't been the only target of the disguised thug last night? He'd have to get the syringe they'd found turned over to the police for analysis.

"Emma ponied the colt out to the half-mile post. She should be back any time." He turned his attention once again to the track, picking up the rhythmic clop of horse hooves in the dirt. "So what do you think? Does Navigator's Whim have what it takes to win the Derby?"

"He's a powerhouse with heart. I've barely tapped his speed potential. Under the right jockey he could take the Triple Crown."

Great, another true believer. Mac gripped the top rail of the fence while he watched Emma, Oliver and Navigator materialize out of the mist like an apparition. For the first time he found himself analyzing the bay colt's stride. Looking for that it factor. The look of eagles in his eyes. Knowing. Confident. Fierce. An old saying in the Bluegrass reserved for winners.

His heart hammered in his chest. There it was, a rush of hope that sent men and women over the edge. Compelling them to move heaven and earth for a chance to bet on a winner. He should turn around and get the hell out while he had the chance. He had nothing at stake in this gamble…but Emma Clareborn did.

Judging by the run-down condition of Firehill Farm in the light of day, she had everything to lose if the colt didn't come through.

Concern embedded itself in his brain and he made a silent

vow to do whatever he could to ensure disappointment didn't destroy her.

Emma reined in her horse next to the gate and dismounted. "He's good and warm, Josh. Take him to the wall this morning."

"You've got it." Josh took hold of the reins while Emma unfastened the buckle on the halter she'd used to pony him and slipped it off.

"Break on the outside rail and move him inside, just like last time. If we get a bad gate pick, he'll be ready to overcome it."

Mac stepped out onto the track and approached Josh. "Rider up," he called. He caught Josh's foot and hoisted him onto Navigator's back.

Josh put his feet into the irons on the flat saddle and gathered the reins in his hands.

"I wish this blasted fog would burn off," Emma said. Leading her pony horse, she headed for the opening in the rail.

Mac followed, watching her tie the leggy black gelding up before moving over to stand next to him.

"Want to do the honors?" She opened her hand to expose a silver stopwatch. Every horse racer's instrument of delusion.

It should have been a simple decision, but he wrestled with it anyway. The track time wasn't going to lie, it was finite, a rock-solid indicator of what the horse was capable of.

"Sure." He plucked the watch from her palm and saw a slight smile bow her lips.

"If I didn't know better, I'd say you'd spent a considerable amount of time around racehorses."

Caution glided through him. Would she have been old enough at the time to remember the feud that tore their fathers' friendship apart?

"It was a long time ago, I was a kid. But you don't forget something ingrained in your DNA."

"Solberg was right then, you're the man for this job. I'm glad you're here."

Mac stared over at her, at the surety in her whiskey-brown eyes as she searched his face with her gaze. His throat tightened. He could easily fall under her spell if he didn't pull back.

He turned abruptly, waiting for the sound of the horse breaking from the far left end of the track.

The fog dampened the swish of the mock starting gate, but there it was, hoofbeats pounding Kentucky soil. He raised the stopwatch in front of him, feeling his heart rate shoot up. Closer…closer…the colt flashed in front of them.

Mac started the clock, listening to the horse thunder down the front stretch and into the first turn.

Emma put her hand on his forearm and shook him. "I told you he's fast. I know he can win."

Her excitement leached into him and he let a degree of the sensation move through his body. Focusing, he turned his head to the right and picked up the hammering of hooves as Navigator thundered his way down the backstretch.

He didn't dare look at the time; instinctively he knew it would be incredible. Better to wait until the colt passed in front of him. Seeing would usher in believing, and then some.

There was trouble. Mac felt it first telegraph through the top rail pipe that ran the entire length of the racetrack. Seconds later Josh's yelp of pain reached out through the fog.

"Something's wrong!" Emma squeezed his arm.

Navigator galloped from the mist minus his rider and shot past them on the inside rail.

Mac pressed the stopwatch and shoved it into his pocket.

"Take Oliver and go find Josh, I'll go after the colt!" Emma said. She ran through the opening in the gate.

Mac turned for the pony horse at the same time he heard her shrill whistle for the riderless colt.

He jerked the knotted reins loose from the rail, untied the pony horse, jammed his foot in the stirrup and climbed aboard. He hadn't ridden in years, but riding a horse was like riding a bike. You never forgot.

Spurring him forward, Mac trotted through the gate and out onto the track. Josh was somewhere on the back turn. That's when he'd felt the vibration of Navigator's impact with the outside rail. He reined the gelding to the inside and eased him into a lope.

A hundred yards around the track the fog vanished, giving him a clear view of the back turn.

Josh lay in a crumpled heap next to the outside rail at the one-mile post.

Worry ground over Mac's nerves.

The kid wasn't moving.

He nudged the horse into a gallop and reined him in just short of the spot where he lay.

"Josh! Can you hear me, buddy?"

Mac bailed off of Oliver and dropped the reins.

Going to his knees, he put his hand on the kid's shoulder.

Josh moaned, rolled to the left and tried to sit up, but Mac held him down with gentle pressure. "No way, stay put."

Mac gritted his teeth, staring at the dazed expression on the young man's dirt-smudged face, but it was the deformity in his right forearm and the protruding bone, that told him Josh shouldn't be moved. He was going to need a trip to the hospital ASAP.

"I gotta catch the horse." Josh tried to sit up again.

Mac pressed his palm into his chest. "Relax, Emma is taking care of it. She'll catch him. You broke your arm. Stay still."

Josh glanced down at his right forearm and went pale.

"What happened?" Mac asked, praying he could get the kid's attention before he passed out cold.

"I couldn't see when I hit the midpoint on the back-stretch."

"The mist?"

"A flash of red light hit me in the eyes—"

"A laser?"

"Could have been. But it must have targeted Navigator too, because he went wide and slapped the rail. I couldn't hang on. I hope he's okay."

Mac looked up and saw Emma and Navigator materialize out of the mist and into the sunlight.

"Is Josh all right?" she hollered the instant she was within earshot.

He waited until she stopped ten feet out, holding Navigator by the reins and trying to calm him down.

"Broken arm. He needs an ambulance, and we need the sheriff. This was no accident. They were targeted with a laser. Blinded. Probably from somewhere in the woods."

Mac swept the grove of dense foliage with his gaze and considered looking for the perpetrator or perpetrators, but the shroud of fog would make it almost impossible to find them. And he had no intention of leaving Emma, Josh or Navigator alone right now.

Emma couldn't prevent her hand from shaking when she pulled her cell phone out of her coat pocket and dialed 911. This was a turn she hadn't anticipated. Whoever was behind the threats against her horse apparently wasn't afraid to hurt his human handlers, as well.

She'd need Mac Titus now more than ever.

"WE FOUND THIS last night after someone attempted to get into Navigator's stall. It could have the man's fingerprints on it." Mac handed the glove encased syringe to Sheriff Riley Wilkes.

"This happened last night?"

"Yeah, just after I arrived around 10:00 p.m. I heard Miss Clareborn scream, booked it to the stable and caught the man trying to run. I tackled him, but he got away. My guess is he wanted to administer whatever's in that hypodermic to her horse."

Mac watched the ambulance carrying Josh pull away and considered his revelation about McCluskie's Derby prospect. "Josh mentioned one of Rambling Farm's horses had some trouble last night, too. Maybe the incidents are related."

"I'll get this to the lab and speak with Chester about it. There's been some trouble at other farms in the area over the last couple of weeks. The horsemen are concerned."

Caution pulled Mac's nerves tight. "Any other horses targeted with lasers on the practice track?"

"Not specifically. But I can tell you two of the reported incidents have been at farms where Victor Dago stabled horses. I'm glad to hear you've been hired as a bodyguard by Miss Clareborn to look after her horse. Keep your eyes open and contact me immediately if anything else happens."

Mac took the business card Sheriff Wilkes dug out of his shirt pocket. "I will, and we'd like to know the results of the toxicology on the syringe's contents as soon as possible."

"I'll put a rush on it." The sheriff turned to one of his deputies.

Mac scanned the paddock and focused in on Emma, leaning against the fence watching Navigator cool down on the hot-walker. He walked over and took a spot next to her.

"Sheriff Wilkes is going to find out what's in the syringe."

"Who would want to hurt him?"

Mac followed her gaze to the big bay colt moving around the circumference of the electric walker's path. "I'd like to try and find out." He watched the horse move, studying him for problems stemming from his contact with the rail.

"He looks good."

"Yeah, not a scratch, but why can't they just leave us alone? Making it in this business is hard enough without someone trying to sabotage you."

He nudged her with his elbow. "I'm not going to let anything happen to him, Emma."

Turning, she gazed up at him, her expression contemplative at best, skeptical at worse. "We're so close to making the cut for the Derby prequalifiers. I need to win the Holiday Classic before I can nominate him in January so we get our shot at the Triple Crown. I need this, Mac. Firehill needs this."

"How bad is it?"

She shrugged her shoulders and shook her head. "Bad enough that I had to ignore the rumors circulating about Victor Dago and his crew and lease my stud barn to the man so I'd have the entry fee to get into the Clark Handicap."

"Has he done anything to you?" Tension coiled inside his body, ready to spring on Dago if he'd hurt her in any way.

"Other than make a few inappropriate comments and giving me the creeps, not a thing. The sheikh sends a check religiously the first of every month. They respect my property and privacy. It's nothing I can put my finger on and I should be satisfied when I put their money in the bank—"

"But something's off?" he said.

"Exactly."

The sunlight had incinerated the fog and it blazed down a streak of copper in a loose strand of her dark hair.

He resisted the urge to stroke it back into place behind her ear. "What kind of rumors are following Dago?"

Her gaze dropped to the ground and she turned back to the fence rail. "Prowlers. Lots of movement after dark. At the Loomis farm, my friend Janet came out of the house to call in her dog and saw a man dressed in black and wearing a ski mask come out of their stable and disappear into the woods.

The next morning she found her dog tied to a fence with duct tape around his muzzle to keep him from barking."

Caution worked through him. "Do they have a Derby prospect?"

"No. They're an anomaly in the Bluegrass—they raise quarter horses, for crying out loud. After that incident they decided to give Dago notice, and he came to me. I needed the money desperately, so I let him in."

He reached out and brushed his hand across her back, a gesture meant to reassure her, but it jolted him hard, and he broke contact. "I'll keep my guard up. No one is going to hurt you or your horse."

"Thanks." She grinned and pulled the lead rope off the fence post next to her then went to take Navigator off the hot-walker.

Mac shoved his hand into his jacket pocket, coming in contact with the stopwatch. He pulled it out and glanced down at the time. His breath hung up in his lungs as he raised the watch out in front of him, like distance from his stare could somehow alter the race time, but it didn't work.

It read 1:56. Three-plus seconds faster than Secretariat's record Derby-winning time in 1973.

Navigator's Whim could win the Kentucky Derby with a time like that.

All he had to do was keep the colt and his determined owner safe long enough for that to happen.

Chapter Three

Mac jolted upright on the cot, unsure what had awakened him. He glanced at the illuminated hands on his watch: 4:35 a.m. Turning his focus to his surroundings, he searched for visual threats inside the barn and saw nothing out of the ordinary. The only noise he heard was the sluice of Navigator moving through the fresh straw bedding in his stall.

Heard. The hearing in his left eardrum had come back one decibel at a time after the shooting, but the healing seemed to have reached a plateau now. It would never be the same, at least that's what the audiologist believed, but he wasn't ready to give up yet.

He laid back and thrust his hands behind his head, staring up at the cavernous ceiling overhead ribbed with giant timbers.

Maybe he could attribute waking up to the sensation of being watched that seemed to follow him every time he entered the damn stable. Whatever it was, he'd made peace with it after clearing every stall twice last night, and poking around in the haylofts for half an hour only to come up empty.

An electric purr coming from the entrance of the barn, reignited the caution in his blood.

He sat up again.

Silhouetted in the doorway by the first hint of dawn was a man in an electric wheelchair. Thadeous Clareborn.

Mac cleared his throat as the chair advanced. He'd changed his last name, but would the old man recognize his face? He smoothed his hand over his hair, snatched the hat from next to the cot and slapped it on his head. Throwing back the sleeping bag, he stood up and prepared to go toe-to-toe with the man who'd, in his father's opinion, destroyed everything Paul Calliway had going for him.

Thadeous stopped the motorized chair. "What's your... name, son?" The question was slurred, each word formed with extreme exertion. A by-product of his stroke.

"Mac. Mac Titus."

The old man grunted and rocked the lever forward, rolling up next to the stall gate. "Emma hire...you?"

"Yes."

He raised his hand and rapped his knuckles on the door. "Good horse?" Angling his head, he stared up at Mac, his eyes narrowing in the shallow light streaming in the barn door.

"Damn straight, Mr. Clareborn."

A crooked smile pulled up one side of his mouth. "Do I... know you?"

Mac's nerves tensed as he shook his head back and forth. It wasn't a lie. He'd been a distant witness to the transactions that had transpired between his father and Thadeous Clareborn. He didn't know the man personally, had only seen him one time. The afternoon he and his father had delivered Smooth Sailing to Firehill Farm, after which Paul Calliway had descended into a bottle of Kentucky bourbon on Christmas Eve and never found his way out.

Glancing over the stall door, concern took hold of Mac's senses. Something wasn't right. Navigator was an animated colt who enjoyed haranguing anyone who ventured close enough to his stall gate for him to nudge, but he stood in the corner now, his head pitched below his withers, his breath coming in long low grunts.

Mac stepped around the wheelchair and opened the door latch. He stepped inside and moved up on the animal. Reaching out he brushed his hand down Navigator's right shoulder, the one he'd slammed into the railing.

"His shoulder's swollen. We better get the vet in." Worry ground through him, bringing his thoughts to Emma, and the devastating reality an injury could cause her and Firehill Farm.

"I'll…go." Thadeous turned his wheelchair and rolled out of the barn.

"Hang in there," Mac said, rubbing the horse's neck.

DOC REMINGTON STOOD outside Navigator's stall next to Emma. "Three weeks, a month. Keep him moving, so he doesn't stiffen up. But no strenuous exercise on that shoulder muscle. It's a deep bruise."

From the pained look on Emma's face, Mac knew the vet's prescription for Navigator was going down like a poison pill. The Holiday Classic was three weeks away and Navigator's fitness level would rapidly decline without regular workouts, thereby diminishing his chances of making the first open qualifier for the Kentucky Derby.

"What about a yarrow-and-mustard poultice?" he asked, recalling the technique his dad had used more times than he could count to speed healing.

A line creased between the vet's eyebrows. "That's an antiquated remedy, labor intensive, but you might get it to draw. It's worth a try."

His only consolation was the look of hope that flared in Emma's dark eyes.

MAC SPOONED ANOTHER square of cheesecloth up from the kettle of boiling water and plopped it down on the piece of plywood they'd been using as a makeshift table since dawn.

Wearing rubber gloves, he spread out the hot cloth and dumped a cup of the yellow paste he'd concocted onto it. He smoothed it around, folded it over to form a pocket for the poultice and pulled off his gloves.

Emma smiled at him as she reached down, picked it up in her gloved hands and headed back into Navigator's stall where she pressed the remedy against his shoulder.

He stepped into the cubicle and watched her over the bay's back. "How are you holding up?"

"My shoulders hurt like crazy and I've got a cramp, but I'm not going to stop."

He liked knowing she wasn't a quitter. The physical strain would have already put an average woman under the table, but not Emma Clareborn. She wasn't the spoiled Kentucky blue blood he'd expected to find living at Firehill Farm. She had grit and substance. Respect stirred in his bloodstream.

Moving around to her side of the horse, he smoothed his hand between her shoulder blades, feeling the knotted muscles. Working them with the palm of his hand, he felt the tension dissipate.

"Better?"

"Yeah, thanks." A tiny shiver rocked her body.

Stepping back he realized he wasn't immune to the effects of the contact either. He left the stall to heat another poultice, his body still buzzing.

"We should walk him out after this one, see if the swelling and stiffness have been alleviated."

"Where'd you learn about this anyway?"

"My dad. When you can't afford to call in a veterinarian every time something goes wrong, you learn to improvise."

"Sounds like he was old-school."

"Yeah." Turning his back to her, he ripped another section off the bolt of cheesecloth and fed it into the kettle. With any luck the treatment would do the trick, but they wouldn't know for sure until they worked him.

Mac looked up and watched Sheriff Wilkes stroll into the barn, remove his sunglasses and push his hat back.

"Afternoon."

"Sheriff." Mac reached out and shook his hand.

He nodded in Emma's direction. "You were right. The drug in that syringe matched the one the vet found in McCluskie's filly. It was a synthetic hallucinogen. Made the horse go plumb nuts in her stall. She's too banged up to race and won't make the Holiday Classic."

Emma came out of the stall and flopped the cold poultice on the board. "That's awful. I know Chester put a lot of hope in her. She has some great track times."

Mac dragged up the piece of cloth from the kettle sitting on the gas camp stove and spooned it onto the board.

"What about prints?"

"None that my technician could find. I wish I had better news, but I don't. My best advice is to stay vigilant. I'm going to send a patrol car by a couple times a night, starting tonight. Maybe they'll get lucky and catch the culprit."

Mac pulled on his rubber gloves and spread out the cloth with his hands.

"Thanks, Sheriff."

"No problem." He slipped on his shades and left the barn.

"Maybe we should get a truckload of motion-sensor lights. Blaze the place out like a Christmas tree if anyone comes near the barn." She arched her eyebrows a couple of times and grinned.

"That's not a bad idea." Mac poured a cup of the poultice on the steaming cheesecloth and smeared it around. "One at the outside front entrance and one at the back would do the trick. I'd also like to put an electronic lock on the stall gate."

"You're serious?"

"Yeah." He stared at her, hoping some of the concern he felt rubbed off on her. This was war, and it could get more intense as the key races got closer. "This person is going to get desperate. The more times we turn back their attacks, the more intense those attacks could become."

"You're scaring me."

"You should be scared, that's what's going to keep you and your horse safe."

He folded the cloth over and she picked it up, moving back into the stall where she applied it to her horse.

"I'll call the hardware store and have them send over the lights tomorrow. And a locksmith to install a lock on the stall door. You can put the lights up, can't you?"

"Yeah." Mac let out a breath and pulled off the gloves.

Any deterrent would help. In fact maybe they should consider rigging the whole damn stable.

"It's cooled off. Let's see if it worked." Excitement stirred in Emma's veins, encouraged by the fact that the swelling was completely gone from Navigator's shoulder. Her racing dreams were alive, well and pinned on the next few moments.

Mac snagged the lead rope and held it out to her.

"You do it," she said. "You're the one keeping my hopes off of life support."

His expression was serious as he clipped the shank on the halter ring and led Navigator out of his stall.

Emma stood next to the gate and held her breath, watching the Thoroughbred move around in a circle beside Mac. His stride was smooth, easy and uninhibited by pain or stiffness.

Relief washed over her. "He's going to be okay! You did it." She rushed Mac and threw her arms around his neck before she'd even thought out the target of her elation.

His chest was a collection of rock-hard muscles, his arms

gentle as he encircled her, lifted her up off the floor and put her back down.

Their gazes locked and his slipped to her lips.

She wet them with her tongue and knew she was in trouble.

Navigator shuffled backward, his ears pitched forward.

Lowering his mouth to hers, Mac hesitated six inches from her lips.

Frustrated, Emma made up the distance and pushed up onto her tiptoes.

Contact. Searing, mind-blowing contact fused them together for an instant before Emma pushed back and struggled to catch her breath. She tried to make sense of her body's overwhelming response to kissing Mac Titus, but she couldn't.

Mac stepped away, pulling Navigator with him as he headed for the barn door. What the hell had just happened? More to the point, why had he let it happen? With every passing minute at Firehill he was being sucked in. And kissing Emma...well, that had been a mistake, he decided, realizing his entire body wanted in on the action and ached for more.

He led Navigator to the hot-walker and clipped him on, then went back to the gate post where he switched the contraption on and climbed up on the fence to watch—get his lust under control, was more like it. He wasn't surprised when she leaned on the top rail of the fence next to him a moment later.

"He looks great, Mac. Thank you."

"You're welcome. We need to rub liniment into his shoulder every half hour and again tonight before it cools down outside. He's going to need a blanket, too. We've gotta keep the muscle warm and loose."

"Hey, why don't you head to the bunkhouse and wash up? I'll keep an eye on him."

"Are you saying I stink?"

Emma stared up at him, seeing a shallow grin arch his

lips, lips she'd like to feel on hers again. "Hardly." In fact she could easily bury her face against his chest and breathe him in for hours on end. "But mustard and yarrow have a way of sticking to you. Better to wash it off while it's fresh. As it is I'll have that smell stuck in my nose for a month."

"Yeah, me too." He climbed down off the fence next to her. There it was again, that rush of desire washing over her mind and body, drowning her resistance in its wake.

"We pulled him back today, Emma. He'll get his shot."

"Yes, he will. Go." She flicked her hand toward the bunkhouse fifty feet to the left of the barn's entrance and let out a sigh when he moved behind her and walked away.

She stared at his retreating backside, at his broad shoulders and the defined muscles beneath his snug white T-shirt. If the air got any more emotionally heated, she swore she'd pass out.

"Breathe, Emma…just breathe." She turned back to keep an eye on Navigator and let her gaze follow him around the endless circle until she felt almost normal again.

Almost.

MAC LAY ON THE COT in the stable staring up at the beams long after midnight.

Emma had made him supper and delivered it to a patch of grass where they ate and tended Navigator's shoulder every half hour. He should have resisted her invitation and indulged in physical activity—pull-ups in the hayloft until his body screamed, or mucking stalls—to break the hold he felt growing between them, but he'd let her get under his skin.

Hell, he was in too deep already and he knew it. Felt it in his bones. Twenty-five years of carrying his father's animosity toward Thadeous Clareborn and the horse-racing business was crumbling like chalk in the rain. But that aversion had shaped his life, shaped who he was and what he needed.

Get in, get out…no emotional attachments.

There was no warning.

No whisper of movement, just the icy pressure of a knife blade at his throat, and the man wielding it standing over him.

Mac's training kicked in, hard, fast, deadly.

He latched on to the attacker's wrist and jerked it up and away.

The blade gleamed sharp in his left peripheral.

Balling his right fist he slammed it back, catching the man in the forehead.

The intruder staggered back and hit the floor.

Mac rolled off the cot onto his belly and snagged the man's ankles just as he tried to stagger to his feet.

Jerking hard, he pulled the thug's legs out from underneath him. He hit the ground again. A grunt hissed from between the other man's lips.

Mac scrambled to his feet and reached for his weapon, determined to detain the invader until Sheriff Wilkes could get there.

Over his right shoulder he heard the slightest sound, the shuffle of footsteps, then the electrical hiss of a Taser gun being fired.

Muscle-paralyzing probes drilled into his back, jolting him into oblivion.

Chapter Four

Emma rolled over in bed, struggling to hold on to the edge of sleep that was slowly being pulled away from her. She shifted again and rolled back toward the nightstand positioned under the window.

Opening one eye, she stared at the numbers on the digital alarm clock: 3:00 a.m.

A hint of cool air breezed in through the tiny crack she'd left at the bottom of her bedroom window. A window that faced the main stable. It was a trick she'd employed as a child and still practiced. Listening to the night, or, to be more precise, to her horse.

The high-pitched shrill of a whinny, followed by a deep rumbling nicker, made contact with her eardrums and shocked her awake.

She pushed up in bed, fully aware now as she focused her attention on the sounds creeping in through the open window.

Again the high-pitched call reverberated on the cold air outside, but this time it raised the hairs at her nape and spurred her to action.

Something was wrong. Something was desperately wrong.

Emma threw back the covers and climbed out of bed, her bare feet hitting the chilly hardwood floor. She stood up, grabbed her robe off the end of the bed, pulled it on and headed out into the hallway. She stopped at the back door long enough to put on her rubber muck boots and flip on the porch light.

Halfway to the barn the sound of Navigator's whinny forced her into a run.

Grabbing a shovel propped next to the barn door, she held it like a weapon and stepped inside. Flipping on both light switches on the wall next to the door, she prepared for battle. The interior of the stable flooded with light.

Navigator spotted her and answered with a grumbling nicker, arching his head over the stall gate.

Her attention fell on the empty cot and the undulating sleeping bag on the ground next to it. Mac?

"Mac!" She dropped the shovel and hurried to his side. Going to her knees, she brushed away the wood shavings as she searched for the zipper. Finding it, she slid in down the entire length of the bag then peeled back the heavy covering.

Air.

Life-sustaining air caught up in Mac's lungs and he pulled it in through his nose, taking deep breaths as he stared up at Emma.

Reaching down she fingered the edge of the duct tape that covered his mouth and ripped it off.

His skin stung like fire where it tore, but he sucked it up.

"What happened?" She rocked back and began to untie the baling twine fusing his wrists so tightly together; he wondered if they'd work again.

"The colt. Is he okay?"

"Who do you think woke me up?" She continued working the knots until she freed his hands. "He's got talent, Mac, but I know he didn't do this. Who did?"

Mac bent and fiddled with the rope binding his ankles. "I

was jumped by a thug dressed in black and his buddy used the Taser on me from behind." He loosened the last knot, shucked the twine off his boots and stood up, then pulled Emma to her feet.

"We need to check him over, make sure he's okay." Striding to the stall gate, he brushed his hand down the horse's face and leaned down, eyeing all four of Navigator's legs.

"We can lead him around just to make sure."

"Yeah. Let's do that. I've been stuck suffocating in that sleeping bag for the last hour. Whoever they were, they had plenty of time to injure him."

Worry laced around his nerves and attached itself to his thoughts. For all his training, he'd been no match for a man with a Taser gun and the element of surprise afforded the intruders by the diminished hearing in his left ear.

He snagged the halter and lead rope off the peg next to the gate and undid the latch. Stepping inside the stall, he caught Navigator, put on his halter and led him out into the center of the barn, moving him in a circle while Emma watched.

"He looks great, Mac. We got lucky."

Frustration clouded his outlook on the situation. "If we got lucky, then what were they doing here?" He turned toward Emma and stopped in front of her. "Take him. I'm going to check out his stall before you put him back in."

She took hold of the lead rope. "It does seem strange if the horse was the target that they'd tie you up like a Christmas package and simply walk away, leaving him unharmed."

Her observation aligned with his thinking as he stepped into Navigator's stall and moved around the perimeter, looking for anything that had the potential to harm him. Nothing.

"It's clear, there's nothing here."

"Good." She led the colt back into his stall and removed his halter. "Your description of the men sounds a lot like the one my friend Janet saw at Loomis Farm. The type that seem to follow Victor Dago around."

He trailed her out of the colt's stall and latched the gate. "Does Dago have a Derby prospect?"

"Not that he's touting, but he does have a nice three-year-old stud colt named Dragon's Soul. He's put down some fast times on the track and he won his maiden race."

Caution worked over him and he considered the idea that maybe the intruders were closer than they'd ever imagined. "I've got a contact in Lexington. I'll give him a call, see if anything comes up on Victor Dago."

"Great. So you were some sort of a cop before you took this job?"

"I worked for the Secret Service guarding dignitaries."

She stared at him for a moment, her eyes narrowed in contemplation. "And that's how you were injured?"

He watched her as she continued to gaze up at him, knowing full well she wanted details. Details he had no intention of giving her.

"Yes." Stepping away, he picked up the sleeping bag and shook off the shavings, then tossed it onto the cot. "I need to get some sleep."

"I'll leave you to it then."

Mac gave her a quick once-over. His gaze focused on the oversize rubber muck boots sticking out from under the hem of her silky robe before trailing back up to the mass of dark hair hanging loose in long waves that fell to her waist. "Thanks for letting this cat out of the bag."

A slow smile pulled at her sweet mouth. "I heard Navigator calling. You have him to thank." She motioned to the horse and turned for the door. "I'll see you in the morning."

"Good night." He watched her walk out the barn door and followed ten steps behind.

Pausing next to the entrance, he leaned against the jamb

and looked after her until she was safely inside the main house via the back door.

The porch light went out and he turned back into the stable, studying the interior. The place was as exposed as a secret with a gossip columnist chatting up the blue bloods. The intruders had simply come in one of the doors. He'd have to limit the access points immediately and consider sleeping in the hayloft over the tack room, which looked directly down into Navigator's stall.

One of the only access points was a permanent ladder rung up the sidewall. The other was a massive loading door in the front of the barn thirty feet above the ground, used to fill the loft with hay. It offered an ideal vantage point.

Mac advanced deeper into the stable, trying to pick up on the thug's path through the wood shavings on the floor. It was a nearly impossible task, but he spotted a faint trail leading to the rear entrance of the barn.

But something bothered him. The men had bought themselves time by using a nonlethal method to subdue him.

Time for what?

He glanced in each stall as he made his way to the back of the stable and stopped just short of the exit. Looking to the left, his stare fell on the ladder leading up into the rear loft. Traces of sawdust were deposited on the first five wooden rungs.

It was possible someone had climbed into the back loft for a bale of alfalfa, but he knew for a fact the grass hay in the front loft was being used to feed Navigator right now. Still, he couldn't rule out the chance that Emma had used the ladder.

Mac grabbed the handle on the massive rear door, slid it shut and put the pin in the latch. For now he was content that his Navigator was safe and asleep in his stall.

EMMA WATCHED MAC TIGHTEN the last bracket on the series of motion-activated lights they had installed at the front and back entry points to the barn. If so much as a stray cat roamed near the entrance, it would be put in the spotlight where Mac could take action.

She let out a long sigh as she stepped back from the base of the ladder he stood on and watched him descend. She liked having him at Firehill. Liked the way he made her feel. The way he deflated the bubble of uncertainty that floated worry in her mind. "The locksmith will be here tomorrow to put a keypad on the stall door."

"Good." He held the screwdriver out to her and she took it, their fingertips brushing in the handoff.

Heat pulsed up her arm and she pulled back before staring up into his face at the knowing smile on his lips.

"Last night, after you left, I searched the stable and found sawdust on the rungs leading up to the rear loft. Any chance you climbed up there yesterday?"

"No. I haven't been up there since they delivered the alfalfa in October. I don't even plan on feeding it until January."

"I've got a sneaking hunch the thugs who jumped me last night may have been hiding up there."

Emma shuddered, unable to fight the uneasiness the creepy revelation generated in her body. There were too many places to hide at Firehill, and they could spend an aeon trying to search every one of them.

"Relax. I'll keep the back door locked up from now on." He grinned at her from under the brim of the brown felt fedora he'd found in the tack room. In fact, it had been hanging in there for as long as she could remember.

"Any more chores?" he asked.

She wanted to roll her eyes and play coy, but it wasn't in her DNA. "As a matter of fact, it's time to put up the Christmas lights around the eaves of the main house. I could really use your help."

His smile faded and hesitation hardened his features. "That's not in my job description."

"Have you got something against Christmas?"

He looked away, focusing on something just over her head before he again met her gaze. "It wasn't the happiest time of the year for me growing up."

"I'm sorry." A mixture of sadness and curiosity congealed in her veins.

"Okay. Well, just think of it as adding colored security lighting."

He lifted his eyebrows in amusement. "You don't like scrambling up tall ladders, do you?"

"Not so much. Come on. I have the light strands untangled and laid out on the back step." She headed for the main house, hearing the aluminum rails of the ladder clank together behind her. "We can have it done before dark."

Just because she loved Christmas and the sweet memories it evoked for her didn't mean that everyone did. She could respect that. Still, she wondered what event in the young life of the battle-scarred bodyguard had given birth to his hostility.

Mac felled the closed ladder, hooked it with his arm and followed her. He remembered the Christmas lights being on at the Clareborn house that December evening when he and his father had driven down the lane to Firehill with their beat-up horse trailer hitched to his dad's Ford pickup, and their last best hope of a horse, Smooth Sailing, in the back. Of unloading the colt in front of the Clareborn barn.

His life had gone downhill from there.

Tension knotted the muscles between his shoulder blades as he willed the memory to expire and leaned the ladder up against the back of the house.

Emma put several coils of lights on her arm. "The hooks are still in place, and the extension cord plug-in is right there." She pointed to the receptacle and unwound a section of the colored lights, then handed him the plug.

Mac took it and climbed up the ladder, dragging the strand with him as Emma uncoiled it from her arm.

By the time they reached the midsection of the house, they had their tandem working system in sync, and he was beginning to get in the mood that went with the physical labor of decorating. It helped, too, that Emma smiled up at him every time she started another row of lights.

Putting another plug into the end of a strand, she reeled off a length of the brightly colored lights, and handed them to him.

Mac took them and started back up the ladder, one hand on the rung, the other grasping the strand.

The initial sound of a single bulb popping just above his head was inconsequential.

Pop! The spray of shattering glass riveted his attention on the bullet hole drilled into the siding on the house.

The next shot splintered the wood a foot above Emma's head.

"Get down!" He lunged for her, kicking away from the ladder and forcing it in the opposite direction.

It scraped down the side of the house and clanked onto the grass.

Snagging her with his left arm, he pulled her to the ground in a tangle of Christmas lights and cord.

Covering her body with his own, he scanned the dense bank of trees and brush a hundred yards from the side of the house, spotting the shape of someone buried deep in the protective foliage.

He drew his weapon, but he didn't have a clear shot. "Do you have your cell?"

"No." His was sitting on the counter in the tack room. Another bullet drilled into the siding halfway between the ground and the overhead eave.

They were pinned down.

Emma struggled to make sense of the situation as she sucked a couple of breaths into her lungs, feeling the weight of Mac's body pressing her into the grass.

Someone was taking shots at them? Someone wanted them dead? Fear pushed chills through her body. She closed her eyes, listening to the whisper of Mac's breath against her hair. Honing in on the sound to prevent herself from being caught up in the wave of panic swelling inside of her.

Mac would keep her safe, he would protect her, with his life if necessary.

"I'm going to return fire as a diversion. When I do, I want you to stay low and head for the back door. Get inside and call 911."

"Okay." She felt his weight shift off her. She scrambled out from underneath him, hearing the decisive crack of gunfire behind her as she half crawled, half ran and ducked around the corner of the house, up the steps and safely through the back door.

She charged the length of the hallway and burst out into the living room, almost colliding with her dad in his wheelchair.

"I called…the sheriff. Who's outside?"

"I don't know who's shooting, but Mac's still out there."

Worry locked her in place as she knelt next to her father, straining to hear what was going on.

No more shots. Silence. Blessed silence. Worry ground over her nerves as she considered the implications.

Either the shooter had been hit, or—

Emma crawled into the dining room, where a window faced the west side of the house.

Her hand shook as she pulled open the drape an inch and stared out on the side yard.

Dusk was settling over Firehill, but in the fading light she saw Mac dart across the driveway leading back to the barn and take cover next to the trunk of an oak tree on the edge of the brushy thicket.

A measure of relief flooded her insides. He hadn't been shot tonight. But he had been shot at some point. Realization surrounded her thoughts as she pulled back from the window and crumpled on the floor to wait for help to arrive.

The horrible scar on Mac's beautiful face was a gunshot wound. He said he'd worked for the Secret Service. The scenario fit. He'd dived to protect another human being with his own body and had taken a bullet for that person, just like he would have taken a bullet for her ten minutes ago.

She swallowed and closed her eyes, trying to imagine the pain he had endured, but it was inconceivable.

In the distance she could hear the shrill wail of a siren. Emma opened her eyes and stood up, seeing the strobe of the police car's lights reflecting against the drapes.

"Emma." Her father called.

"Yes." She moved into the living room. Concern brushed her nerves, as she stared at her dad, at the stricken look on his face and the piece of paper in his hand.

"Give this to…Wilkes. It's why…I called him."

Reaching out she took the paper and stared at the string of text that had been cut from a secondary source and strung together word by word to form a sentence.

Don't race your horse or next time I won't miss.

"Where did you get this, Dad?"

"It came in the mail…this afternoon. Sam brought it in just before she left…for the day. I opened it…twenty minutes ago, and called the sheriff. It's a threat against…Navigator."

There was fear in his eyes as he worked to speak.

She put her arm across his shoulders. "Don't worry, Mac and I won't let anything happen to him." Her reassurance seemed to calm him. She carried the note into the kitchen, where she pulled a large Ziploc bag out of a drawer and slipped the note inside before going back into the living room.

"Where's the envelope it came in?"

"On the desk. No...return address."

Moving to the rolltop, she found the plain white envelope next to the stack of mail and added it to the bag. "I'll take this to the sheriff."

Her dad nodded and she headed down the hall, flipped on the porch light and exited the back door, coming face-to-face with Mac and Sheriff Wilkes at the west corner of the house. They were deep in conversation.

Mac looked up as she approached. "Emma. Are you and your dad okay?"

"Yes." She turned to face Wilkes. "Here's the note we got in the mail this afternoon. My dad called you the moment he opened it."

Wilkes reached out and took the plastic bag, holding it up where the porch light illuminated the crude message.

"It's the second one today. Brad Nelson over at Cramer Stables received one this morning."

"Derby prospect?" Mac asked, feeling a measure of concern enter his bloodstream.

"Yes. He plans to nominate his horse Whiskey Fever for a spot in the Kentucky Derby."

"Were there any potshots taken at him?" Mac asked, knowing that if one of the gunshots had been a foot lower it would have hit Emma.

"No. But with any luck you scared him off and he won't try this over at Cramer Stables. Did you by any chance get a look at him?"

"No. He took off the moment I put a slug in the tree. But

Brad Nelson would be wise to get some security in place around his horse, just in case he tries this over there. Whoever is behind these attacks is serious. It's only a matter of time before someone is seriously hurt, or worse."

"I agree," Wilkes said. "And a heads-up. Some of the surrounding farms have banded together and put up a reward for the capture of whoever is behind the threats and attacks against their horses."

"Is that right?"

"Twenty-five thousand dollars and climbing. I'll file my report and get this letter to the lab tonight after the forensics team takes a look at the scene for slugs or shell casings. I'll drop by in the morning if they find anything."

"Thanks, Sheriff. I've got to go check on the colt."

Mac turned for the barn, anxious to make sure the horse was okay. One thing the evening's events had made clear—Navigator wasn't the only animal being targeted in the Bluegrass. But how did last night's intruders and Mac's subsequent stint trapped in a sleeping bag play into any of this?

The shuffle of footsteps behind him slowed his pace, and he was glad when Emma fell in next to him.

"Hey, where are you going? We can't let a couple of stray bullets dissuade us. We've got Christmas lights to hang."

He chuckled, pulled up short and turned to look at her in the last glimmer of Kentucky twilight.

"Do I look like the Grinch, Emma?"

"Um…maybe a little around the eyes."

"I want to make sure the colt's settled for the night, then I'll help you finish the lights."

"Okay."

Mac headed for the barn again with Emma keeping stride next to him. Glancing across the paddock, he spotted several men standing in the doorway of the stud barn, looking into the deepening darkness.

"Do Victor Dago and his crew ever work their horses?"

"Yes. Every other day they get the practice track in the morning and I take the afternoon slot."

He mulled her answer as they approached the barn entrance and the motion light clicked on. They entered the stable together and Emma flipped on the overhead lights.

Mack walked to Navigator's stall and the horse immediately put his head over the gate for a scratch.

"He likes you, you know," she said.

Mac stroked the bay's forehead and glanced over at her where she leaned against the wall next to the gate.

"He's a horse, Emma. They like anyone who takes care of them and slips in an occasional carrot. The finer details of an interpersonal relationship don't exist."

Navigator bobbed his head and snorted, blowing a fine mist of green moisture at him.

She busted out laughing as he wiped off the back of his hand and shook his head. "Navigator loves a challenge. Even if that challenge is to convince you he wants an interpersonal relationship." She grinned, studying him intently in the glare of the lights.

"I figured it out tonight. I figured out how you got that scar."

He watched her mood turn serious and contemplated the sudden direction the conversation was taking.

Emma took a step closer to him, staring at the deep furrow that cut along his left jawbone from ear to chin.

Her body went on autopilot as she raised her right arm and touched his face, stroking her hand along his jaw. He didn't pull back, he didn't flinch, he just met her unwavering stare with one of his own.

"You saved someone's life and almost lost your own. That's how you got this?"

"Yes."

Her heart was pounding out of her chest by the time her palm reached his chin and she let her arm drop to her side.

"How long ago?"

"Six months."

"Working for the Secret Service?"

"Yes."

"Can you tell me what happened?"

"No."

"Oh." A myriad of questions flitted through her mind. Who, why, what, where, when and how, but her final summation ended with a level of surety she felt lock in place between them.

She trusted that he could protect her and her horse from just about anything, and he'd be willing to give his life if necessary.

Chapter Five

"Mac Titus is ex-Secret Service. He's out on medical leave after nearly having his face blown off by a bullet meant for a foreign dignitary visiting Louisville six months ago."

Agent Renn Donahue rocked back in his chair and took the intel report from Agent Conner. "So what's he doing at Firehill Farm?"

"Trying to get his edge back. He was referred to Firehill by the Solberg Agency, a bodyguard service out of Louisville that mentally rehabilitates agents who've been through an incident so they can rejoin their respective employers if possible. More than likely he's there to protect a high-valued horse."

"What's his medical history look like?"

"He has extensive damage to his eardrum. He's almost totally deaf in his left ear. The assailant's bullet entered below his earlobe and traveled the length of his jawbone before it exited through his chin. He protected the dignitary with his own body when the shooting started and took the bullet at close range."

Agent Donahue jotted the fact down on the bottom of the page next to Mac's service photo. Military-style haircut, clean shaven…a damn far cry from the unshaven, long-haired man in the surveillance still taken in the stable at Firehill. It was an identity crisis, plain and simple, but life-threatening incidents did funny things to a man's soul, and his nerve.

"Any chance he'll return to his post?"

"I don't know, I'm not a doctor. But the service requires all your senses be at a hundred-and-ten percent. His never will be again."

"Looks like the odds are against Mac Titus. Anything else, Agent Conner?"

"Not that I could access. The details of the attack are encrypted."

Strange. A knot firmed in Donahue's gut. "I'll take the late shift in the surveillance van tonight. You need to spend some time at home with your new wife."

"Thank you, sir." Conner pulled a sly grin as he turned for the office door and Renn refocused his attention on the paperwork in front of him, searching for the name of the dignitary Mac Titus had nearly been killed protecting.

Sheikh Ahmed Abadar.

Caution seeped into his bloodstream. The NSA had been listening to chatter from Abadar for months. He was the cornerstone of their investigation at the farm.

So was Mac Titus's presence at Firehill a coincidence? An odd twist of fate?

Or something more?

MAC LEANED INTO THE RAIL and scanned the entire perimeter of the practice track, concentrating on the wooded area adjacent to the backstretch before picking up the progress of the colt galloping into the clubhouse turn with Emma on his back.

It made him uneasy to see her astride the big bay colt in her breeches, goggles and helmet. The sooner they found a new gallop boy to replace Josh, the better. In the interim she seemed determined to work the colt herself and damn the danger that could be lurking in the woods.

He sucked in a breath of crisp morning air and tried to

still the agitation circulating in his veins. He cared about the horse…and the woman on his back.

Navigator blitzed by, his powerful hooves pounding the rich Kentucky soil.

Mac focused on the sweet round curve of Emma's bottom, pushed up above her sloping back in classic jockey form. A low whistle hissed between his lips. The woman could ride.

In the peripheral vision on his right, Mac saw Victor Dago approach the rail and he turned for an instant to acknowledge him before resetting his gaze on horse and rider.

"He's fast. He'll win the Classic," Victor said.

"Yeah. If we can keep him safe and running until then." Mac shot Victor a quick glance, trying to gauge his reaction. His eyes continued to follow the progress of the pair on the track.

"What happened last night? My animals didn't take to all of the commotion."

"Someone took three shots at Miss Clareborn and myself." Again he slipped a glance at Dago, and witnessed his genuine look of surprise.

"I've heard rumblings of sick horses and threatening notes."

"Where?"

"Keeneland Horse Park. I buy my crew breakfast at the Iron Liege Coffee Shop once a week. The horsemen talk. I listen."

"Any names come up?"

"No."

Mac watched Navigator and Emma pass in front of him for the second time and turned to face Victor. "If a name happens to surface, I'd like to hear it. Some strange things have been taking place on the farms with derby prospects, and I suspect someone is trying to up their odds of winning. Any chance you have a Derby horse?"

Victor's eyes narrowed for an instant and his brows furrowed. "I've got one possibility, Dragon's Soul, but I'm not sure if he'll go to nomination this year."

Mac picked up horse and rider in the backstretch and leaned on the rail. "Keep an eye on your horse, and I'd appreciate it if you'd advise your crew about what's going on. Sheriff Wilkes is tracking some leads right now. He may want to talk to them."

"No problem." Dago pushed back. "Tell Miss Clareborn if she'd like to use my gallop boy, Rodriguez, on his off days, to let me know."

"Thanks, I'll do that." Mac nodded and watched Victor walk away, unsure what to make of him. If he or anyone in his stable were behind the attacks, Mac sure hadn't wrangled anything out of him by perpetuating the idea the sheriff was tracking solid leads. There weren't any.

He watched Emma rein Navigator in and slow him to a canter as they jogged down the front stretch and into the first turn for a final cooldown lap.

Pulling his cell phone out of his jacket pocket, he punched in the number of his buddy in the FBI's Lexington office.

Every Thoroughbred trainer in Kentucky needed a license acquired through the horse-racing commission. It also required an FBI background check. He wanted to know what was in Victor Dago's.

Emma reined in Navigator and flowed with the rocking-chair rhythm of the powerful horse underneath her. She let her knees act as shock absorbers in the stirrup irons as she kept time with his gait.

He'd barely broken a sweat in the four-mile gallop she'd just put him through. He was in peak condition. Ready to run. Ready to win.

Focusing on the final turn out of the backstretch, she tugged the reins again and shifted him down into a fast trot. The

Holiday Classic was two and a half weeks away. A lifetime for something to go wrong. Thank goodness she had Mac looking out for them.

On the right, she picked up a flash of movement in the brush.

Navigator saw it first and shied to the left.

The first bone-jarring jolt almost unseated her.

Half a dozen doves took flight out of the bushes and fluttered into the air inches above her head.

Navigator shot forward and broke into a run.

Emma sat down on the saddle, pulled back on the reins and squeezed him with her legs to bring him under control. "Easy. Just a couple of birds." She reached down and patted his neck, feeling the tension dissipate in his body and control return. Her heart rate had slowed by the time she eased him into a fast walk and aimed for the opening in the rail, seeing Mac hurry out onto the track to meet them.

"What happened out there?"

"A cove of doves took flight and spooked him."

"Nice recovery, but he could have dumped you. Hurt you."

"I know."

Mac caught one of the reins and walked the pair through the opening and into the paddock, where he stopped the horse and Emma jumped down. "He looks good."

"He's ready to run. I could have taken him around again at a full gallop."

"Conditioning wins races." He pulled up on the two leather straps of the cinch and released it from the buckle while she took off the bridle and put on the colt's halter.

In a matter of minutes, Mac was clipping him on the hotwalker for a thorough cooldown.

She gathered up the equipment and headed for the stable, satisfied with the morning's workout.

Mac joined her a minute later in the tack room and busied himself wiping down the saddle and bridle with an oiled rag.

"Where'd you learn to ride like that?" he asked.

She glanced up at him. "I've been riding since I was a kid. My dad used to let me exercise some of the horses until I got too tall."

"Victor Dago offered to let you use his gallop boy if you need to."

She stared at him, considering how calm she felt with him next to her. Watching the skilled manner in which he cleaned the dirt and horse sweat off the flat saddle as if he'd done it a hundred times before.

"I'll pass. Rodriguez likes the whip and Navigator doesn't. I contacted Sam McCall, the trainer over at Rambling Farms and asked if they had an extra gallop boy, being as their Derby prospect, Ophelia Mine, isn't in training right now. They're sending jockey Grady Stevens over on Thursday. I've heard good things about him. I'm going to ask him to ride the colt in the Holiday Classic."

Mac cleaned the last section of the leather and slid the flat saddle onto its metal pin protruding from the tack room wall. "That's good news. With everything that's going on around here, I worry about your safety."

She met his dark blue gaze and felt her cheeks warm under the intensity. Begging for a distraction, she picked up the feed bucket on the counter and turned for the grain sack.

"I trust Navigator. I trained him from the moment he hit the ground." She put the bucket down into the sack and scooped up a gallon of sweet feed. "He's a good horse. Not a malicious bone in his body." She straightened, flipped up the handle on the pail and set it on the counter. "He'd never do anything to hurt me."

"It's not him I worry about. It's whoever seems determined

to force an injury. It's as simple as spooking him like the birds just did on the backstretch. Something like that could end in disaster."

She sobered, knowing that her argument would mean little to a frightened horse with the power to crush anyone in its path, including the one who'd cared for him from the time he was born.

"You're right. I tend to give him human qualities and he's a horse." She glanced away and reached for the feed bucket topped off with Navigator's morning ration of grain.

Caution locked on his nerves. "Hold on." Mac reached out and covered her hand on the lip of the bucket. "Let me see that."

He stepped closer and released her fingers, still feeling the touch afterward.

He sifted through the top layer of sweet feed and felt his brain go numb. He gritted his teeth as he scooped up a handful of the multi-grain concoction and held it out so she could look.

"See the tiny white crystals?" He isolated one with his fingernail.

"Yes."

"It's Butazolidin."

Emma's eyes went wide as she stared at the feed in his hand and back up into his face. "Bute?"

"Yeah. How long have you been feeding out of this sack of grain?"

"I took delivery the day before you got here. I've been feeding it for over a week. Do you know what this means?"

Mac's heart jumped in his chest. He saw tears well in Emma's eyes. Her prequalifying for the Derby dreams were crumbling and there wasn't a damn thing he could do about it.

He dumped the handful of drug-tainted feed back into the bucket and reached for her.

She moved against him and he pulled her into his arms, feeling her body quake.

Mac closed his eyes, working through the problem in his head and mentally trying not to memorize every curve of her body pressed against his in the process. Butazolidin, known as bute in racehorse circles, was banned. Any racehorse caught with it in its system on race day could be disqualified, even barred from competing at racetracks around the country.

He pushed back and grasped her upper arms. "Call the vet. Get him out here for a drug test. We don't know how long it's been in the feed. There's a chance we found it in time, and it'll work its way out of his system before the race."

Emma brushed her hands across her eyes, taking her tears with them. Mac was right. They didn't have any idea when the bute had been mixed into the feed. It could have been done a day ago. "I'll call him now and we should contact Sheriff Wilkes. Other farms could be affected by something like this and not even know about it until it's too late."

"I'll call Wilkes." Mac pulled his cell phone out of his jacket pocket.

She hurried out of the tack room headed for the house, the telephone and a measure of hope.

MAC AND EMMA WATCHED Doc Remington tweezer the white crystal out of the sweet-feed bucket and drop it into a test vial filled with clear liquid.

He capped it with his thumb, shook it and held it up to the light.

Within seconds the liquid turned yellow.

"It's Butazolidin, all right. Do you want me to test your horse, Emma?"

"Is there any way to judge by the blood sample what the percentage of bute is in his bloodstream?"

"Yes. It won't change anything, but we can get a better read on how long it's going to take for him to purge it from his system."

"And if it's positive, Doc, what are the chances we could treat him with a diuretic mash, green tea and pasture grass to speed up the process?" Mac studied the veterinarian, hoping he'd remembered the layman's prescription correctly along with the ingredients.

"What's in the mash?" Doc Remington studied him from behind his glasses for a moment before he poured the liquid out of the vial onto the ground and put it back into his test kit.

"Oats, cabbage, carrots, lettuce, asparagus and a bit of molasses. We'd steep green tea and add it to his water supply."

"I don't see why that couldn't work. It'll get his kidneys working overtime to flush the drug out, and the pasture grass will help, as well. Give him plenty of exercise. Where'd you learn a remedy like that?"

Mac felt the muscles tighten between his shoulder blades. They were moving into territory he'd rather leave uncharted. "I heard it as a kid and remembered it."

Doc Remington shook his head and picked up his kit. "Bring the horse over to the truck and I'll take a blood sample."

He turned for his pickup. Mac followed.

"Only one man I know ever used those techniques with any success. An old horse trainer named Calliway, Paul Calliway, if I remember correctly. He was one of the best horsemen in the Bluegrass. Don't know what ever happened to him, but he was always coming up with the damnedest cures. The funny thing is, they usually worked."

Mac tensed, cocking his head slightly to the right to judge

whether or not Emma was in earshot, but she'd already turned away and headed for the hot-walker.

It had been years since he'd last heard his father's name out loud. A name he'd been more than happy to abandon when his mother remarried and he took his stepfather's last name. "We'll keep you in the loop on his progress. Emma has him entered in the Holiday Classic. What are his chances?"

"It's a long shot. But he might be clean by then." The vet opened one of the side boxes on his truck and reached inside.

Mac glanced up just as Sheriff Wilkes rolled down the drive and parked next to the vet's pickup.

"Morning, Doc. Mac." Wilkes nodded. "It's a damn shame we can't catch these guys. Did the vet confirm your suspicions?"

Mac shook the sheriff's hand. "Yeah. Someone put Butazolidin in Navigator's feed sack. We're going to try to clean him up before the race on the twenty-fourth."

"I hope it works, for Emma's sake. In the meantime, I've got my deputies doing robo calls to every farm in Fayette County advising them to check their feed for the drug."

"Any forensics come back on the shooting last night?"

"The slugs were from a .22, virtually untraceable, and the prints on the envelope and letter matched Thadeous, his nurse, who brought in the envelope from the mailbox, and Emma's. We didn't find anything on the letter Brad Nelson received."

Mac turned slightly and watched Emma lead Navigator to the rear of the veterinarian's pickup. "We'll catch a break. Somewhere, somehow, someone will make a mistake, and we'll catch him."

"I hope so. There's a lot of expensive horseflesh at risk in Fayette County." Sheriff Wilkes turned for his car.

Mac couldn't agree more, but it was the bay colt and his

owner who occupied his concern right now. He skirted the front of the vet's pickup and made his way around to the back, where Doc Remington was just capping the hypodermic.

"I'll rush this, Emma, and give you a call in an hour or so with the results."

"Thanks, Doc." She raised her gaze to meet Mac's and flashed him a hopeful smile, before leading Navigator toward the hot-walker and the remainder of his cooldown.

The vet stowed the blood sample. "I'll be in touch." Doc climbed into his vehicle, fired up the engine and pulled away.

Turning for the barn, Mac tried to still the curiosity that churned in his mind. Doc Remington had known his father all those years ago and still remembered him? How was it possible that the veterinarian's image of Paul Calliway was so totally different from his own?

His cell phone rang. He pulled it out of his coat pocket and glanced at the caller ID—FBI.

"Hey, Doug. That was quick. Have you got something for me?"

"I couldn't find the man's name in our Kentucky database. If he's holding a trainer's license here, it could be a fake."

Mac stopped in his tracks and stared at the barn. "What kind of penalties go with an offense like that?"

"A fine, possibly imprisonment, maybe even a ban from the sport."

"Thanks."

"No problem." Doug hung up.

But it was a problem. A problem for Emma Clareborn. A problem he wasn't sure he could fix.

Chapter Six

Mac closed his cell phone, trying to reconcile the caution creeping through his system with the facts circulating in his brain.

If Victor Dago had used a fake license to lease Emma's stud barn, could it explain the thugs dressed in black who seemed to follow Dago around like a goon squad? Were they there to make sure his secret went unchallenged?

It all seemed a little too cloak-and-dagger for a horse race, but desperate men did desperate things. He could attest to that. Maybe Dago was behind the attempts on Navigator and the other Derby prospects in Fayette County?

"Mac!"

The sound of Emma's voice jolted him out of contemplation, and he glanced up to see her waving from the railing facing the hot-walker.

Worry pushed his pace to a jog as he headed straight for her and stopped next to her, his stare going to the colt as he walked the merry-go-round.

"What's wrong?"

"Relax. I just saw you freeze up over there and wanted you to snap out of it. I think the colt's going to be okay. We're going to pull him out of this, Mac. I know it."

"How are his legs?" he asked, eyeing Navigator's stride.

"Cool to the touch."

"Good. We'll have to keep a close eye on them while the bute purges from his system. He'll be more susceptible to injury for a while. Any aches and pains he might have will be exacerbated."

"Thank you, by the way, for spotting the Butazolidin in his feed. I never would have caught it in time. I would have shown up at the Holiday Classic and he would have flunked the drug test. Of course, only after winning the race, losing the purse and our entry fee, then being disqualified, not to mention the harm to the farm's reputation."

She looked sideways at him, and he contemplated telling her what had rooted him to the earth a moment ago, but he couldn't be certain, not until he'd had a chance to snoop around. The rent the extra stable brought in was vital. If Victor knew his secret was about to be exposed he could bolt, leaving Emma scrambling to make up the revenue shortfall.

"There you go again."

Mac resisted the need to reach out for her. She lived her financial life on the edge, but always managed to have a smile on her face.

"What do you say we saddle a couple of horses and take the colt out to graze on pasture grass in one of the lower fields next to the creek for an hour or so?"

"That's a great idea. I've been planning to pick out a Christmas tree from the grove and drag it home, but I've been too busy with the horse to get it done."

Mac gritted his teeth, but didn't protest. If she wanted to cut a *Tannenbaum,* he'd help, or stand guard against another incident like the one that transpired the last time he'd helped her spread some Christmas cheer.

Gunfire.

"I'll saddle Oliver," he said.

"Catch the bay gelding, too. I'll ride him. His name's Dandy."

Mac turned from the fence, spotting activity outside Dago's barn where five men warred with a single black horse as they tried to put a bridle on him.

"Damn," Mac swore under his breath, watching one of the men swing a rope and slap the animal across the chest. The horse reared, pawing the air with his front hooves before coming back to ground where the tug-of-war continued.

Emma held her words of warning, watching Mac turn and head for the ruckus like a man with a mission.

She fell in behind him, her nerves fraying between the moment she saw him pause on the edge of the fracas, and when he reached out to the animal.

One by one, Victor and his men stepped back.

The horse turned his focus on Mac now, ears tilted forward, sides heaving beneath his shiny black coat slick with sweat from the fight.

Emma swallowed, fearing for the man who'd given her fresh hope. He was no match for the colt. She fought the urge to look away and held her breath. Dragon's Soul was notorious for striking out with his front legs. She'd watched Dago and his grooms do battle with the horse from the first moment they'd stepped foot on Firehill Farm.

If anything happened to Mac...

"Easy. Take it easy." Mac reached out to the frightened animal, remembering the moves his dad had used to draw a horse in and establish trust.

Cupping both of his hands, he bent his arms at the elbows and pulled them toward his body in a coaxing motion. His dad had called his method the language of horses. "Speak horse with your body language and the animal will respond."

Dragon's Soul took a step forward, then another, until he was standing directly in front of him.

Mac reached out and put his palm on the front of the horse's head, holding it there until he calmed.

"Does he do this every time you try to put the bit in his mouth?" He focused on Dago.

"Yeah. Every time."

With his other hand, he slipped his index finger into the corner of Dragon's Soul's mouth and felt along the sides of his upper and lower teeth, coming in contact with several that were as sharp as a razor's edge. Studying the horse's physique, he could see the weight loss from the horse's inability to properly chew his feed.

"You need to get the vet out here, Dago, and have his teeth filed down. They're so sharp it's causing him extreme pain when you bridle him, and when he tries to eat. He's already dropping weight."

"Rahul, go and call the veterinary clinic in Lexington, get them out here as soon as possible."

The groom let go of the rope in his hand and headed for the stable.

"Thanks." Dago nodded and unhooked all but one of the lead ropes attached to the horse's halter. He led Dragon's Soul back toward the barn.

Mac studied the group of men for a moment, memorizing their faces before he turned around and saw Emma watching him from well outside the circle of action.

She met him halfway and they fell into stride next to one another.

"The Titus touch. Where'd you learn to horse-whisper like that?"

"Is that what it's called?" He headed into the stable and stepped into the tack room.

"Yeah. It's become a really popular method of training and understanding horses, using their own language."

He pulled a couple of halters down from a hook on the wall, and grabbed two lead ropes. "Can we talk about this later?"

"Sure." Emma took the halter he handed to her and stared

at him for a moment longer than was comfortable. She had a way of seeing into his soul and he didn't want her to get any closer.

"Don't you find it unusual that Victor Dago didn't know what was wrong with his animal? I mean, even a layman knows horses periodically need to have their teeth filed down for maximum health." He met her gaze, hoping like hell the diversion turned the conversation in a different direction.

"He does a lot of odd things that don't play well for a horseman, much less a trainer, but everyone has their own methods, Mac."

He headed out of the tack room and together they exited the north end of the barn, where they took a left and walked toward the pasture gate to catch the horses.

Knowing what he did about Victor Dago, he'd have to take it down a notch to keep from arousing Emma's suspicions. At least until he had something definite to tell her about something that could impact Firehill in a negative way.

Still, he had to keep his trouble-ahead radar from bouncing off the questions inside his head, and sounding a loud warning that couldn't be ignored for long.

EMMA REINED IN DANDY at the edge of the grove of trees and dismounted into shin-deep grass that rustled in the cool afternoon breeze.

She moved around to the horse's head and took Navigator's lead rope from Mac while he dismounted beside her.

"The hobbles are in my saddlebag."

Mac led Oliver around to the other side, flipped up the flap on the leather pouch and pulled out the three sets of leg hobbles she'd tied herself. The devices were made of soft cotton rope with a slip knot on each end that went around each of the horse's front ankles. They would allow the horses to graze freely, but not give them the latitude to run off.

"Nice job." He glanced up at her.

She smiled, taken by the tilt of his head as he studied her for a moment, then retrained his eyes on her hobble handiwork from under the brim of his hat.

The afternoon sun shone down on the pristine side of his handsome face, while the other half hid in the shadow, much like he did, in her estimation.

Her chest tightened in a funny sort of way she found pleasant. She found another focal point in order to squelch the sensation and stared instead at the vast grove of conifers she and her father had planted twenty-five years ago.

Mac Titus intrigued her and frightened her all at the same time, and she wondered if she'd ever be able to truly draw him out into the open.

"We'll need this." He held up a small hacksaw she'd put into the saddlebag and moved around to hobble Navigator, before he unclasped the lead rope.

"Have you spotted a Christmas tree yet?"

"Patience. I like to take my time. Besides, the good ones are at the center of the garden."

He grinned at her and shook his head, as one by one they hobbled the other two horses and removed their bridles so they could graze on the grass uninhibited.

"This is a beautiful spot, Emma."

She pointed to a path and fell in step behind him as they climbed the base of the knoll and followed the trail into the dense stand of blue spruce, pine and noble fir.

"Yes, it is. I use to ride out here all the time."

"And you don't anymore?"

"Not so much since my dad's stroke. I haven't been able to find the time to do the things I used to do. It helps that he has a private nurse now; it has freed me somewhat, but I still worry about him and don't leave the farm too often."

Mac ducked under a low-hanging branch and held it back for her until she passed and moved on ahead of him.

"Do you see one you want to take home and dress up like a Christmas tree?"

"Impatient, aren't you? Just stay on the path, we're almost there." Excitement forced her to pick up the pace now that she was in the lead. She'd never brought a man out here before, out into a place she grew up calling her secret garden, but she wanted Mac to experience its magic just the same.

Tension knotted the muscles between Mac's shoulder blades as he scanned the dense layers of trees surrounding them, and looked for anything that posed a threat.

He didn't like feeling so exposed. Someone could easily take another round of shots at them and he'd have a hard time isolating their location. Hell, if he weren't tagged up with Emma on a clear path, he'd be as lost as a draft horse on a Thoroughbred racetrack.

The lay of the land progressed up in elevation with each step, and he relaxed slightly at the sight of an opening in the curtain of green at the top of the knoll fifty feet in front of them.

Closing the distance between himself and Emma, he emerged into the small clearing and stepped in front of her as he searched for danger around the perimeter of the perfect circle he found himself standing in.

"So what do you think?" She brushed past him and moved into the center of the circumference. "Isn't it great?"

Mac turned all the way around before he joined her in the middle. "You and your dad planted all of these trees?"

"Yeah. We put in the first ring of seedlings the spring I turned five, the year after my mother died. And another ring every spring after that until my dad's stroke."

He had to keep his teeth clamped together to keep his mouth from gaping open as he turned around, staring at the graduated layers of trees all rustling in the breeze and giving the small clearing the feel of an arena, with row upon row of cheering fans surrounding the center. "It's amazing, Em."

"What did you call me?"

He turned to face her, realizing in his state of awe, he'd let an affectionate abbreviation of her name slip.

"Em. I called you Em. I'm sorry."

"Don't be." She stepped closer to him and gazed up into his face. "Only my dad calls me that, but it sounds good coming from you."

Mac's heart skipped a beat as he stared at her lips, then back up into her whiskey-brown eyes. The moment seemed to blend them together like a smooth drink. He reached for her, slipped his fingers under her chin and raised her mouth to his.

The air around them was cool, but her lips were hot against his. He closed his eyes and deepened the kiss, pulling her body to his with a need that burned through him like fire.

Heat exploded in his veins when she pressed her body to his and locked her arms around his neck.

He ended the kiss and lowered her to the soft grass, where he pulled her on top of him and stared up into her face.

Emma worked to get her ragged breathing under control. "I knew this place was special, but that. That was—"

Cupping the back of her head, he pulled her lips to his again, cutting off her words.

She kissed him back. Giving. Taking. Working to satisfy the need building inside of her inexperienced body.

He broke the kiss and rolled to the left, pulling her underneath him, where he kissed her again, before relenting and slowly rolling off her. He pushed up into a sitting position. "I shouldn't have kissed you without asking."

Rolling onto her side, she sat up and faced him. Reaching out, she cupped his scarred jaw in the palm of her hand.

"I'm not complaining. I know where my boundaries are, and if you'd have crossed them just now, I'd have told you." She swallowed, enjoying the pulse of heat that ricocheted between them like lightning.

She wanted him to kiss her again and again. She wanted to explore the myriad sensations flooding her body. Sensations she'd never explored to their ultimate conclusion with any man.

In the distance the purr of an engine caught her attention. "Do you hear that?"

She saw Mac turn his head slightly to the right, as if the movement could somehow dial in the sound.

"No. What is it?"

"It sounds like a motor. Maybe to the east, down by the creek on the other side of the knoll."

Mac stood up and helped her to her feet.

On a hunch, Emma reached up and snapped her fingers inches from his left ear. He didn't even blink. "Why didn't you tell me, Mac? Why didn't you say something? The shooting damaged your hearing."

"It'll come back." He stared down at her with a look of certainty in his dark blue eyes.

She sobered, realizing the effect profound hearing loss would have to have had on his ability to do his job for the Secret Service.

The grind of the engine grew louder over the whisper of the wind in the pines.

"Come on." She grabbed his hand and headed for the trees on the other side of the clearing.

Mac could hear it now, the hum of an engine, as clear as rain. "Is anyone supposed to be out here?"

"No."

Caution hedged his pace through the pines. Pulling to a stop, he grabbed Emma and held her against him as a pickup truck roared past their location on the edge of the tree line. From the cover of a massive spruce, they watched the truck make its way along the narrow dirt road running parallel to the creek.

"Where does the road go?"

"It dead-ends at a gate that leads to the lower pasture. My father fenced it off years ago because of the shallow caverns carved out in the limestone by the water. He didn't want any of our horses to fall through the weak topsoil. He dynamited the largest cavern's entrance so no one would get hurt."

"Do you recognize the vehicle?"

"Yeah. It belongs to Victor Dago."

Mac took Emma's hand and guided her along several feet inside the protective layer of trees. "Would Dago have any reason to be out here?"

"No. His lease doesn't include access to Firehill lands, with the exception of six stalls in the stud barn, the paddock and the track."

They circled the top of the knoll, stopping at a vantage point a hundred yards from the spot where the truck rolled to a stop at the closed gate.

Mac pulled Emma to the ground, watching as the man behind the wheel climbed out of the pickup and looked around in every direction before walking toward the gate.

"That's one of Victor's grooms," Emma said.

"Yeah, his name's Rahul. He's the one who went to call the vet for Dragon's Soul."

"He's the only one who speaks English besides Victor."

Caution stilled Mac's body as he saw the man stop, then turn with a jerk. He stared in their direction as if he knew they were there and was trying to pick them out of the trees.

"Don't move a muscle, Emma," Mac warned, feeling the hairs on the back of his neck bristle.

The air charged around him as he watched Rahul hurry

back to the truck, climb in, fire the engine and turn the rig around. But rather than speed off, he braked to a stop in a cloud of dust and revved the motor.

"What's he doing?" Emma whispered.

"I think he may have spotted us." Mac gauged the amount of protection around them, glancing at the mature pine perimeter six feet in front of them. If Rahul came into the grove on foot, he could easily be taken down. But if he found a way to penetrate the tree line with the pickup they were in real trouble.

The transmission ground into gear. The pickup lurched forward, traveling back along the dirt road headed in their direction.

Tension knotted Mac's nerves as he watched Rahul move closer, then slow down.

Reaching under his coat, he unholstered his weapon and drew a line of sight on the pickup as it flashed through the trees and drove right past their position.

Emma sucked in a breath and rolled over onto her back. "What the heck just happened?"

Mac glanced over at her, still listening to the drone of the truck as it went back the way it had come. He holstered his weapon. "I don't know."

"Rahul's driving lesson 101, maybe. Did you hear the way he ground the gears?" Emma asked.

"Maybe." Mac tried to reason out the scenario they'd just witnessed. What if Emma was right? What if Rahul was just trying to learn to drive a stick shift? He estimated the man to be in his early twenties, and in light of Victor's possibly bogus trainer's license, maybe Rahul's was, too.

"Come on, we better get your Christmas tree cut and back to the farm."

Emma scrambled to her feet. "I know just the one I want."

Mac followed her back into the clearing where he retrieved the saw he'd dropped on the mashed-down grass in the exact spot where he'd kissed her unrepentantly.

His heart rate ticked up as he watched her peruse an eight-foot-tall blue spruce, then shake her head and point at a well-shaped noble fir.

"This one," she said.

"Are you sure?"

"Yes, that's it."

He watched her smile and rub her hands together in anticipation. His heart expanded in his chest as it filled with a measure of her childlike excitement.

Three minutes of sawing and the fir was felled and being dragged back down to the pasture, where the horses grazed on bluegrass and his emotions returned to seminormal.

He planned to make another trip out here to find out what lay beyond the closed gate. He wanted to know for sure what Rahul had really been up to.

A self-imposed driving lesson, or a distraction to hide something nefarious? Something just beyond the locked gate?

Chapter Seven

Emma's cell rang just as Mac was dismounting Oliver to open the pasture gate leading back into the farm's main paddock.

She pulled the phone out of her pocket, glanced at the screen and felt her stomach pucker.

"Hello."

"Emma?"

"Hey, Doc." She glanced at Mac as he paused next to the gate to watch her, his concern unavoidably tied to hers.

"I've got the results of Navigator's blood test."

"How bad is it?"

The veterinarian's long pause at the other end of the line made her heart turn in her chest and she waited for the guillotine to drop on her dreams.

"I'm not going to lie to you Emma. The levels in Navigator's system are high. Butazolidin binds with proteins in the blood at a rate of 99 percent. He most likely ingested upward of 800 micrograms a day from the tainted feed for over a week. If you do get him clean, one percent of the bute could still be present in his tissues."

Emma finger combed Dandy's mane, trying to soothe her disappointment with the gesture, but it wasn't working.

"What about the drug test he'll be required to take at Keeneland? Will that disqualify us?"

"It wouldn't show up on the drug test on race day, but he's

going to need an injection of thyroid-stimulating hormone to counteract the bute. It competes for the same cellular binding sites as the hormone does. Your only chance is using Mac's remedy for purging his system with natural diuretics, but I have to tell you honestly, it's a long shot."

Emma rubbed her forehead with her fingertips and tried to swallow the news with an ounce of dignity. "How soon does he need the thyroid injection?"

"As soon as possible, or his conditioning will suffer, if it hasn't already. We can give him another shot at the end of Mac's treatment to make sure he's working at his full capacity."

"Sounds like a plan, Doc. Can you come by tomorrow afternoon?"

"I have a three o'clock opening."

"We'll take it. I'll see you then." She closed her phone and slipped it into her jacket pocket. "It's bad, Mac."

In a few steps he was next to her, helping her down off her horse and gathering her in his arms.

She leaned into him and closed her eyes tightly against the sting of tears behind her lids.

They were so close. So close to an end shot at the Derby. Who knew something like this could derail everything she'd worked so hard for?

"Don't give up, Em," Mac whispered against her ear. "You have to hang on and it'll work out. I promise."

She wanted to believe him. To hold on to the hope in his assessment of the situation. She pulled in a deep breath and pushed back, staring up into his face, at the way his features softened as he gazed down at her. At the long scar on his handsome face that probably carried with it more discouragement than she'd ever known.

"You're right. If I can hope that the colt will win the Derby if given the chance, then you have every right to hope your hearing will return someday."

She reached up and brushed the side of his cheek. He closed his eyes for a moment, reopened them and focused on her.

"We'll make it happen. With the mash and green tea, we can purge the drug from his system. I've seen it work."

She nodded in agreement, but her awareness had shifted to the feel of his body against hers, to the warmth and pleasure it generated in her veins as they pressed together between the two horses.

Her gaze dropped to his lips, then back up to his eyes. She wanted to kiss him again. To experience the surge of emotion and curiosity it had awakened inside of her. She watched a muscle flex along his jaw as he gritted his teeth.

"Emma," Mac said, transfixed in a moment he was unwilling to resist. Her invitation was subtle but effective. He lowered his mouth to hers.

Contact.

Searing heat flared, scorching his nerves and churning his blood to white-hot.

A low nicker from Oliver brought Mac out of the fever and he ended the kiss. Staring down into Emma's face, he watched her eyes flick open, her chest rising and falling in a heightened rhythm that matched his own.

"Come on. We've got a lot of work to do." He reached up and pulled the rope they'd used to drag her Christmas tree home off of Oliver's saddle horn and dropped it.

"Yeah," she said, nodding as he returned to the gate latch, slid the bolt action pin and pushed the sixteen-foot panel open.

He was out of line. Kissing Emma Clareborn, repeatedly, didn't play into his career plan and as much as he enjoyed doing it, it had to stop.

Determined, he worked to curb the desire in his body and

lead Oliver through the gate and over to the front of the stable, where he looped the reins on a hitching post, and went to work unsaddling the horse.

Emma tied Dandy up next to Oliver, then led Navigator into the barn.

Mac worked the cinch, pulled the saddle and blanket off of the horse and deposited them on the hitching rail. About to turn and unsaddle Dandy, he caught a glimpse of movement in the paddock across the way.

Rahul stood behind the six-foot-high fence, staring through the gap between two of the rails. He immediately turned around and headed for the Dago stable.

Caution surged in Mac's blood as he watched the man's progress until he ducked inside the main door of the stud barn.

"Hey."

The sound of Emma's voice returned his focus to the job at hand.

"What are you looking at?"

He unsaddled Dandy while she brushed Oliver out. "Rahul was across the way in the paddock. I think he was waiting to see who came in out of the pasture." He watched her shudder, then continue working the brush over the horse's coat a second later.

"That's just creepy."

"Yeah, but it makes sense. He knows someone saw him out at the southeast gate. He knows this is one of only two ways in and two ways out."

"And now he knows it was us?"

"Yes." Mac couldn't alleviate the measure of concern that locked onto his thoughts. If Rahul's business on Firehill's land was benign, he'd have no reason to want to discover who'd been a witness to his trek out there this afternoon.

"After we put the horses away, will you help me drag the

Christmas tree to the back of the house, and soak its base in a bucket of water?"

"Yeah." He glanced up, watching her stroke the brush across the horse's back, and remembered the feel of her lips on his. She was the most beautiful woman he'd ever kissed, but it was her grit that intrigued him the most and aroused curiosity in his veins.

Keeping his distance from her from now on wasn't going to be easy. In fact, it would probably be the hardest thing he'd ever have to do.

EMMA CHOPPED ANOTHER BAG of carrots on the makeshift cutting board Mac had rigged up next to Navigator's stall and scraped them into the five-gallon bucket they were mixing the mash in.

Mac reached in up to his elbow and stirred the vegetables into the mix with his hand.

"Thank God he's eating this stuff." She wrinkled her nose at the sulfur smell of the green cabbage, which had permeated the interior of the stable.

Mac glanced up at her and grinned. "It's the molasses. Suckers them into eating it every time."

She didn't doubt it. Horses loved the sweet taste of the iron-rich sugar by-product.

"I hope this works. Is it another one of that guy Calliway's remedies?"

Mac inwardly flinched. "You heard Doc Remington mention him?"

"Yeah. I also caught your reaction. Have you heard of him?"

"Hasn't everybody?" He pulled his arm out of the mix and slicked off the excess with his other hand. "I'm going to clean up at the bunkhouse, then we'll feed him again and make more green tea."

"Okay."

He watched her open another bag of asparagus, lay the spears out neatly on the cutting board and slice through them with a razor-sharp knife. He turned and left the barn, trying to calm the agitation that circulated in his body. Hearing his father's name twice in a day left him feeling one step ahead of disaster.

Nothing but trouble had ever followed Paul Calliway around until the day he died. At least he and his mother had been liberated that day.

Mac turned the knob on the bunkhouse door and walked into another disaster.

"I'll be damned." The place had been trashed. Every drawer in the dresser hung open. His clothes had been tossed out and heaped on the floor. The mattress on the bed was shoved off its foundation, and the kitchen had been ransacked.

Annoyed, he headed for the sink, stepping over the debris, careful not to disturb anything. The odds that Sheriff Wilkes could find any telling evidence was unlikely, but he was pretty sure he knew who'd done it.

Turning on the faucet, he ran his molasses-covered arm under the tap and washed off the sticky stuff. He shut off the water, snagged the dish towel off the rack and turned around.

Emma stood in the doorway of the bunkhouse, her mouth hanging open. "Oh, no!"

"It happened while we were gone this afternoon." He put the towel back on the rack. "We can call Wilkes, but I'd bet whoever trashed the place wore gloves."

She stepped inside and closed the door behind her. "Is anything missing?"

Mac scanned the room with his gaze and finished the sweep by looking her in the eyes. "My guess is, someone was looking for information on me. Fortunately, I haven't spent much time in here and I always keep my ID with me. We should consider questioning Victor Dago and his crew."

"Rahul?"

"He did beat us back here by half an hour. He had plenty of time to pop in for a look."

"Some look." Emma shrugged. "I'll help you clean it up."

"Thanks. But it'll have to wait until Navigator is secure."

She turned back for the door and opened it, but didn't step outside. "If you do question Victor and his crew," she turned back around, "be careful, Mac."

"I will." He followed her outside into the early-evening twilight. "I got some information this morning from a source I know in Lexington."

She fell in beside him as they walked toward the barn. "Oh. Sounds serious."

"Hold up for a minute." He stopped and turned toward her, grasping her upper arms in his hands. Through her jacket, he felt her body quake and second-guessed his decision to tell her about Dago. Still, she had a right to know.

"I have a buddy who works for the FBI." Tension threaded along his nerves. "I had him check Dago out through the racing commission's background-check system."

Emma stared up at him, her eyes widening in increments that matched her concern. "I knew it. I've felt it from the minute I leased him the stable. He's a crook."

Mac shook his head. "I wish it were that simple. We'd call Wilkes and he'd arrest him and haul him away." He pulled in a breath. "Victor Dago is carrying a phony trainer's license, Emma."

Her brows furrowed. "The license he showed me to rent my stud barn is bogus?"

"Yes."

"That doesn't make any sense. You fabricate a name and

information so you can rent a barn and run a second-rate racing stable for an absent sheikh? I'm not seeing any benefit here."

She had a point.

"Come on. Let's get back to the stable, we can talk there." Mac glanced around to make sure no one was within earshot of their conversation and headed for Navigator's six-o'clock feeding with a knot in his stomach and unanswered questions on his brain. Questions like, what did Victor have to gain?

MAC ADJUSTED HIS PILLOW and rolled onto his left side so he could look down into Navigator's stall from his perch in the loft above. It was the perfect setup for spotting anyone who risked a venture into the stable to try and harm the horse. In addition, the locksmith had shown up around 8:00 p.m. and installed a keypad on the stall door.

If anyone tried to jimmy it, he'd hear them and be able to take action well before they got to the colt.

He closed his eyes, focusing on the sounds of the night. The weak hum of crickets fighting the cold, the rustle of the straw bedding as the colt moved in his stall and a mechanical sound he couldn't identify.

He opened his eyes and sat up, perusing the cavernous barn.

Turning his head to the right, he listened again, just picking up the whisper of a sound that seemed to be coming from somewhere in the loft.

Caution skated over his nerves. He rolled off the sleeping pad underneath him, and pushed it back along with the sleeping bag. Leaning close to the wooden decking with his right ear to the ground, he held his breath, hearing the mechanical grind again, only louder this time.

Using his hands he dusted away the layer of grass hay that

covered the area where the noise seemed to be coming from, and revealed a half-inch gap between the decking boards.

Mac reached into his coat pocket and pulled out his mini flashlight. Turning it on, he aimed the beam into the crevice.

"I'll be damned," he whispered as the light's beam picked up the sheen of a skinny piece of coaxial cable that had been lain in the groove.

Following it with the flashlight beam, he tracked it into the back of the loft, brushing away the hay, until he reached a spot where a void had been chiseled out and a small power supply was tacked into the hollow, flush with the wood.

This was the handiwork of a pro.

He turned around and followed the line back up to the edge of the loft, but he didn't need a visual to confirm what he already knew.

Someone had installed a surveillance camera in Firehill's barn.

To spy on Navigator's Whim? It certainly explained the sensation of being watched that he'd experienced from the moment he'd set foot in the stable. But who in the hell was on the other end watching? And why?

He grabbed his sleeping bag and flopped it over the lip of the loft, covering the tiny pin camera at the other end of the cable.

"Lights out."

Tension knotted his muscles as he rocked back on his feet and stood up.

The two men in black who'd used the Taser on him and left him all tied up had probably been there to service the cameras.

His gaze locked on the hayloft at the other end of the barn. Could there be another one?

That could explain the sawdust he'd seen on the rungs.

Hell, they were probably watching him right now.

Mac killed his flashlight and shoved it into his coat pocket. He walked to the ladder and climbed down. The images from the camera would give its viewer access to every aspect of Navigator's routine. His training schedule, his feeding schedule. When and for how long any one person stayed in the barn.

Hanging close to the row of stalls, he worked his way along the wide corridor to the back of the barn and scaled the ladder.

He reached the loft and pulled out his flashlight, then turned it on. To his right a narrow slot opened behind the three tons of alfalfa hay in the loft. On his left, the stack was flush with the wall.

Mac angled sideways and pushed into the space, working his way to the end, where he stepped out onto an open area of the decking. Dropping to his knees, he brushed away the scattered hay and exposed a narrow crack running from the back of the loft to the front.

"Bingo." The light hit on a shiny piece of black coax cable. "Camera two." The thugs had had trouble with this one, and incapacitated him with the Tasered so they could fix it. He planned to give them more trouble right now. He killed the flashlight and dug his pocket knife out of his jeans pocket. He opened the longest blade and stuck the knife into the closest bale, where he bored a small hole in the densely packed alfalfa.

Relying on the light coming from the open tack room door, he found the cable again and worked the knife blade into the crack and under the cable. He dislodged it.

Prying it out, he snagged it with his fingers and ripped it loose, then stuffed the camera lens into the bale of alfalfa hay.

Next time the thugs in black showed up to fix their blank surveillance camera, he'd be ready.

EMMA EASED THE BACK DOOR of the house closed and stepped out into the first light of dawn as it broke on the horizon. She was anxious to assess Navigator's progress on Mac's remedy, and more than anxious to see him.

She fingered her braid at the nape of her neck and pulled it free of her coat before sliding the zipper up against the morning chill. Taking the walkway in the back, she noted the layer of frost on the grass. She would have to harrow the track this morning to break through the thin layer of frozen soil before she let Navigator take his exercise laps at eight o'clock under his new jockey, Grady Stevens.

Glancing up, she spotted Mac in the doorway of the barn, casually leaning against the jamb. He somehow looked right standing there. In fact, he looked at home anywhere on the farm, and if he wasn't there in the capacity of a bodyguard for Navigator, he could certainly be there in the capacity of a horse trainer. He had the know-how and the skills to be great. A measure of comfort adhered to her nerves.

"Good morning." She stopped in front of him, catching a glimpse of tiredness around his eyes along with bloodshot whites. "Rough night?"

"You have no idea." He shoved the brim of his hat back and stepped away from the frame. "I made a discovery last night that could explain how and why someone has been able to get close to the colt."

"Really?" She followed him into the barn and went to take a look at Navigator. "Tell me you caught them and you have them hog-tied out back."

He grinned and shook his head. "Not quite. But I did find two surveillance cameras. One hidden in each loft. It's hard to say how long they've been in operation."

A chill jolted her body. She rubbed her hands together to generate heat and dissipate the feeling of violation scrubbing around her insides. "I hope you smashed them."

"Not a chance. I covered one, and gave the other a permanent view of the inside of a hay bale. I figure whoever installed them will come back to fix them—"

"And you'll be able to catch them?"

"If things go as planned."

Concern fired through her and she leveled her gaze on him, unsure why the idea of Mac confronting the person or persons who could be responsible for trying to injure her horse, made her anxious. It was, after all, the reason she'd hired him in the first place.

"I think we should call the sheriff. Maybe his department can find evidence to link them back to someone."

"Maybe. But I prefer a more direct approach."

"That's what scares me, Mac. Have you forgotten that someone tried to shoot us? What if they try again and they don't miss next time, like the note threatened?"

"Relax, Emma." He reached out and touched her arm, sending waves of heat up her skin. "I'll be careful."

"Let's get him out on the hot-walker this morning to warm up while I harrow the track. His new jockey will be here at eight."

She turned and headed for the door, frustration bubbling up inside of her at his nonchalant attitude toward bullets. She paused at the door long enough to glance over her shoulder at him.

He stood with his hands on his hips, right where she'd left him, a quirky grin on his mouth and his gaze firmly locked on her. She left the barn shaking her head. She would never understand the male bravado. Maybe that was what made it so sexy, and on Mac, so blasted irresistible.

Mac snagged the halter and lead rope off the hook next

to the stall gate and pressed in the lock code, 315. The latch released. He pulled the door open and went into the cubicle.

"Hey, you ready to run today?" He rubbed his hand along the colt's neck for a moment before haltering him and leading him out of the stall, through the barn and out to the hot-walker.

The morning air was icy, a fact that worried him. Cool conditions could lead to injuries if the colt wasn't properly warmed up. Emma was correct to heat Navigator up on the walker before he took the track.

He clipped the walker chain to the halter, took off the lead rope and went back to the post where he flipped on the power switch setting the contraption into motion.

In the distance at the far right end of the track, he heard the John Deere's diesel engine turn over and fire up with a couple of cranks. Mac headed for the rail to watch her make the six to ten laps around the oblong track with the harrow behind the tractor to break up the soil. A hard track surface could injure Navigator's legs.

Mac heard the RPMs over-rev as she steered the tractor forward, heading for the inside rail, churning a trail of dust in her wake.

Reality took hold as he watched the tractor pick up speed and barrel past him. "Slow down, Emma," he whispered under his breath. "You're going too fast."

The tractor went wide into the clubhouse turn and veered hard to the left.

Mac's heart twisted in his chest.

Something was wrong.

He charged out onto the track. "Emma!"

The ancient John Deere plowed into the rail at the top of the turn.

Support boards splintered.

Stressed metal groaned as it stretched and snapped, sending a violent jolt through the entire top rail.

Mac broke into a run, watching in horror as the unleashed tractor vanished over the embankment and Emma's scream pierced the cold morning air.

Chapter Eight

Panic pinned Emma in place as the nonresponsive steering wheel slipped in her hands.

She braced for impact into the railing and spotted the massive poplar tree in front of the runaway tractor.

Jump. She had to jump.

The tractor launched down the slope and smashed head-on into the tree.

Her teeth rattled in her head and she felt herself being propelled forward. Tossed like a sandbag by the impact.

Falling, she was falling, careening off the tractor seat.

She hit the ground, landing on her belly.

The air was forced out of her lungs. She saw stars for an instant.

Disoriented, she tried to judge her position next to the still-running piece of equipment with the diesel engine noise hammering in her eardrums somewhere over her left shoulder.

She tried turning to the left, but she was locked in place by her booted foot, which was wedged in the narrow gap between the front tire and the tractor's frame.

Less than a foot above her head she could hear the relentless grind of the tractor's massive rear tires.

The ground vibrated beneath her forehead and realization pushed a scream up her throat.

She grabbed for something, anything she could hang on to, to keep from being pulled into the spinning tire.

Mac. Where was Mac? She'd seen his face for an instant when the tractor had roared past his spot at the rail.

Pain burned across the back of her scalp, the intensity increasing with every passing second.

With her right hand she reached up and locked her fingers around the base of her braid trying to relieve some of the pressure, but it was hopeless. It was caught under the rotating tractor tire and she was being reeled in.

Her foot gave a little in her boot, threatening to pull out and send her headfirst into the tire.

She tightened her grip on the tractor frame and hung on, praying Mac would get to her in time.

Mac crested the edge of the slope and lunged down the embankment, fighting the panic in his system as he assessed the situation.

Emma had been thrown from the tractor and was now wedged between the front and rear tires, but only the rear ones were spinning, digging deeper and deeper into the soil just above her head.

Kill switch.

He leaned into the tractor and hit the red button to cut the power to the engine, but it didn't die. Like a scene from a horror movie, the giant tire continued to rotate, inching Emma in by her hair.

Mac dug into his pocket, yanked out his pocketknife and pulled a blade open. He dropped to his knees next to her.

Getting as close as possible to the bite of the tire, he sawed back and forth across the thick rope of hair.

It gave as he cut the last strands.

Emma's head popped up. She pulled hard and dislodged her foot, leaving her boot stuck in the tractor, and rocked back onto her knees.

Mac stood up, pocketed his knife, locked his arms around her and dragged her away from the John Deere.

Together they collapsed on the slope and he pulled her against him, stroking the back of her head as he stared at the beast he'd been unable to shut down.

"Are you okay?"

Shudders racked her body and he held her, feeling his own heart rate return to normal.

"I think so." She pulled back and looked up at him. She had dirt smudges on her face, tears in her eyes and a scrape on her forehead where the pressure on her hair had forced and held her to the ground. She had never looked more beautiful.

"Tell me what happened."

"It just took on speed. I turned off the ignition key and hit the kill switch, but it wouldn't stop. The steering wheel popped going into the clubhouse turn and I had no control." She sucked in a deep breath, sobered and brushed her hand across her eyes, leaving a streak of mud behind.

Mac's throat closed and he warred with the surge of emotion boiling up inside of him.

His mission at Firehill wasn't just about a horse anymore. Tractors didn't go kamikaze on their own. Someone had to have sabotaged it. Someone who knew that Emma and only Emma harrowed the track every other day.

"Stay put. I'll go crimp the fuel line to shut it down." He settled her on the ground and headed for the tractor, its rear wheels continuing to dredge a furrow now six inches deep and still digging.

Who had that kind of mechanical know-how?

He popped the metal side panel on the engine compartment and flipped it up. Spotting the fuel line, he folded it over, cutting off the supply of diesel fuel driving the monster. The engine sputtered and clattered to a stop.

He released the rubber line and stared inside the compartment. It was a grimy old tractor, like the one that had belonged to his dad. The one he'd learned to hot-wire so he could bypass the ignition switch in the dual-start system.

Tilting his head, he visually located the wires attached to the kill switch. The last fail-safe way to kill it. "I'll be damned." This was literally an accident waiting to happen.

In his peripheral he saw Emma stand up and dust herself off then approach the tractor with a wary look in her eyes. "Did you find something?" she asked from next to him.

"The kill-switch wires have been cut." He stepped back and turned toward her, watching her finger what was left of her hair over her right shoulder.

"I'd bet someone also tampered with the carburetor's governor and filed the steering column pin so you'd lose control."

"This is getting scary, Mac."

He met her gaze. "I'll catch whoever did this. No one is going to hurt you, Emma."

She stepped closer and he put his arms around her, hoping like hell he could honor his vow and keep her safe from an unknown enemy. An enemy who could be watching them right now.

"Come on, let's take care of the horse, then we'll call Wilkes and file a report so the crime will be documented."

"Okay." She pushed back and fell in step next to him.

"By the way, I'm really sorry about your hair."

"I'm not. You did what you had to do. Besides, I've been thinking about getting it trimmed. I just didn't know it would be this soon and with a pocketknife."

"Maybe later you'll let me even it up with a pair of scissors. I can cut a straight line."

"You'd do that?" She glanced over at him and he enjoyed the easy smile on her lips.

"Sure. In fact, I've been thinking about having mine cut, too. It's been overgrown for too long." He pulled off his hat and raked his fingers through his collar-length hair a couple of times.

It was time for a change. He hadn't seen a barber since the shooting. Somehow, letting his hair grow unabated for the past six months had been an extension of the anger he'd felt inside at the loss of his hearing, and his identity as a Secret Service agent.

Now, somehow, it no longer seemed to matter.

"I'll recut yours, if you'll cut mine."

"Deal," she said.

Mac glanced up, seeing Dago, Rahul and another one of the grooms jogging down the front stretch toward them.

"Miss Clareborn, we heard the commotion. Are you okay?"

"I'm fine, but the tractor isn't." Emma steeled herself, trying to compensate for the uneasiness she always experienced in the presence of Victor Dago.

"Any chance you can fire up your Kubota and harrow the track this morning?"

"Sure." He nodded to Rahul, who spoke to the other groom in Arabic.

The groom turned and headed for their stable at a jog.

"Thanks," Emma said, watching him bob through the opening next to the hot-walker. "It'll probably be a couple of days before the John Deere can be rescued and fixed."

"I understand," Victor said glancing toward the embankment.

"Maybe we could get Rahul to harrow tomorrow morning. We'll pay him." Mac stepped closer, seeing an opening to question Rahul's abilities behind the wheel, whether it be a pickup on an off-limits corner of the farm, or a Kubota tractor.

"Rahul is just learning to drive. I don't trust him with the tractor until his skills improve, but I'll instruct Karif to harrow again tomorrow morning and every morning until your equipment is working again."

"Thank you," Emma said. "I appreciate that."

"Come on, we've got an overheated horse to saddle before eight o'clock and you need to get cleaned up, doctor that raspberry on your forehead." Mac steered Emma toward the opening in the railing and around the hot-walker, where he flipped off the power switch at the post and snagged the lead rope.

"Learn anything back there?" she asked, dabbing at the dirt on her face with the back of her coat sleeve.

He followed her line of sight to the two men making their way back to the stud barn.

"Yeah. Rahul can't drive for beans."

She smiled and shook her head. "So you think his joyride down by the southeast gate was legit?"

"I didn't say that." Tension knotted the muscles between his shoulder blades as he moved in to take Navigator off the hot-walker, still trying to figure out how he could question Rahul about his mechanical abilities without arousing suspicion.

AT 8:35 A.M. EXACTLY, Mac pressed the counter on the stopwatch and watched Navigator blitz down the front stretch into the first turn.

Emma put her hand on his arm where it rested on the top of the railing.

A streak of excitement fired through his body, bringing his stare down to the seconds as they clicked off on the timer in his left hand. "He's fast this morning, Emma."

"He's fast every morning, Mac." She turned and shot him a glance before putting her attention back on the colt thundering down the backstretch.

Mac closed his eyes and turned his head a little to the right, listening to the sound of hooves pounding dirt and the rhythm of the horse's short bursts of breath as he labored around the backside of the clubhouse turn.

He opened his eyes; his heart rate ticked up.

Navigator accelerated into the homestretch and flashed past them on the inside rail. Mac pressed the stop button and held out the clock: 1:54. His breath caught up in his throat. "I'll be damned, he just shaved two seconds off his own record."

Emma smiled over at him. He'd just turned into a giddy kid, judging by the wide grin on his face, and the way he continued to stare at the time, look away and stare again.

"The week before you got here, he ran it in 1:53." She watched him sober on the news, trying to decipher his hot-and-cold reaction, but Mac Titus was a complicated man.

"I'd be lying if I didn't tell you I was skeptical about your claims, but not anymore. The colt's got heart."

She glanced away, watching Grady slow the horse into the turn for his run out. She knew someone else who had heart, even if he didn't know it himself.

"I'll go mix up his mash if you'll unsaddle him and get him on the hot-walker."

"Okay." Mac watched Emma turn for the barn with a slight smile on her lips and stared after her until she stepped inside the stable door. He turned back around, picking up the horse and rider's progress in the backstretch. Still clutching the stopwatch in his hand, he looked at it again.

For the first time in his life he truly understood his father's sickness, and unfortunately, he also knew it was contagious.

EMMA RAN THE COMB through Mac's hair one last time and snipped a couple of hairs she'd missed along his nape. "Looks good."

She stepped back as he stood up and pulled off the towel from around his shoulders. Her pulse quickened as she stared at his bare chest while he put the towel down on the chair in the tack room and snagged his shirt from off the counter.

Diverting her gaze, she focused for an instant on the scissors in her hand before looking back up at him as he did the last button on his shirt. She swore she was wearing desire, because she could feel it in the heat on her cheeks.

Mac gave her a sly grin that did little to alleviate the problem.

"You promised. Cut it straight off in the back, even with the shortest section." She handed him the comb and shears and turned around.

His first touch was gentle, almost hesitant, as he put his hand on her head and eased the comb through her hair.

Emma closed her eyes, feeling him became more proficient with each stroke, working the strands until they were free of tangles. She heard him let out a long, tense breath behind her, and she tried to hold perfectly still for him to begin the cut. "It's okay, Mac. It doesn't have to be perfect. Just good enough to get me by until I can make it in to a salon."

Mac stared at her mass of hair as light from overhead lit up the strands of copper streaking through it. What had once brushed the waistband of her jeans now hit just below her shoulder blades.

He swallowed and tried to erase the sexy image in his mind of shoving his hands into it and pulled her mouth to his.

"This isn't like clipping a mane, or combing a horse's tail."

"Just do it. It'll be fine."

He focused on a single span of hair that was longer than the rest. "The sides are already even." Raising the scissors, he snipped through the hair, smoothed it with his hand and stepped back. "Done."

She turned around and grinned at him. "Thanks. I'll wait around for Doc Remington and feed Navigator another bucket of mash. Why don't you go check out your haircut in a mirror?"

"I'll do that." Mac picked up his hat off the counter, thought better of it and hung it back up on the hook where he'd found it. He left the tack room feeling like a changed man and headed for the bunkhouse, determined to take his reformation a step further.

"He looks good, Emma. Continue to feed him the mash and keep him moving. I'll run an analysis on this sample and give you a call on Monday."

"Great, Doc." Emma glanced up and spotted Mac in the doorway of the barn. At least it looked like Mac, but not the one who had left the tack room less than half an hour ago. This Mac was clean shaven, sexy as crazy and headed straight for her.

"Doc. How's the patient?"

The vet turned and stared at him, his brows drawing together. "Mac. I didn't recognize you for a minute without all that hair and scruff on your chin."

Mac grinned, showing a row of even white teeth.

Emma felt heart palpitations clear down to her toes. "He cleans up really good." She met his dark blue gaze. Her throat tightened. She pulled in a breath and shrugged off the pull of electricity she felt arcing between them.

"How's his track performance?" Doc asked while he dug into his kit.

"Broke his own record this morning," Mac said stepping closer to watch the vet load the hypodermic with thyroid hormone.

"You don't mind if I share the mash recipe with a couple of other farms, do you?"

"Do they have Derby prospects?"

"Yes. A colt over at Sundance Farm and one at Calumet

were both fed enough Butazolidin in their sweet feed to reach the same toxic levels as Navigator."

"Go ahead and pass it along. There isn't a prospect that can even come close to his speed times, bute or no bute." Mac glanced at Emma and watched her smile.

"Old Calliway would be proud." Doc administered the medication to the horse, capped the syringe and put it back into his kit.

Every muscle in Mac's body tensed, but he worked through the turmoil the vet's offhand comparison had evoked. He'd never been one to deny credit where credit was due.

"He'll need one more dose of thyroid hormone once his system is clean, but we'll cross that bridge after I see some results on the blood test."

"Thanks, Doc." Emma walked the colt around then put him back into his stall. She closed the gate and glanced up at the thermometer on the wall before she followed Mac and Doc Remington outside into the warmth of the afternoon. She only hoped it remained this warm until the Holiday Classic at Keeneland.

Together she and Mac watched the veterinarian climb into his pickup and pull up the driveway. "That was good of you to pass the mash remedy along."

"Save your adoration. We don't know if it's working yet." He cast her a sideways glance with a devil-may-care smile attached; it was all she could do to resist the need to run her hand along his clean-shaven jawline.

The drone of a vehicle dragged her attention away from Mac and she saw Sheriff Wilkes's car pull into the farm. Gravel crunched under his tires as he braked to a stop, shut off the engine and climbed out.

"Afternoon, Emma. Mac." He tipped his hat. "Dispatch forwarded your call about the accident this morning. Where's the tractor? I'd like to take a look at it."

"Still down over the embankment on the clubhouse turn of the track. The crash came close to killing Emma." The words churned up caution in Mac's bloodstream and he realized just how vulnerable she was, how vulnerable they all were until they caught whoever was responsible. "I'll take you out there," he offered.

"I'm going to stay with the horse, rub him down and wrap his legs." Emma took off for the barn. She had no desire to look over the scene right now. In fact, she wasn't sure she'd ever trust that damn tractor again.

"I THINK YOU'RE RIGHT. It looks like the kill-switch wires have been intentionally cut. I'll send one of my CSI people out here to get some pictures and I'll file a report, but without an eyewitness to the tampering, I'm not sure my department has any recourse."

"Have things quieted down on the surrounding farms?"

"No. The robocall we put out on the tainted feed produced a handful of owners with the same problem you have. I've got my deputies asking questions, but nothing unusual has cropped up." The sheriff put his hat back on. "Keep me posted if the incidents continue."

Mac fell in next to him as they made their way toward the track's exit. "What about security? Did any of the farms hire security?"

"As a matter of fact, a couple of them did, and they haven't reported any more problems."

"Good. That should narrow the field to a couple hundred, but at least we know these thugs have their ears to the ground, and know which farms have hired help. Maybe I should start carrying my weapon in plain sight. Maybe they'll get the message and leave Firehill alone."

"It couldn't hurt, Mac."

They reached the opening, exited the track and walked to

the sheriff's car. "By the way, the reward for capturing whoever's behind these attacks went up to fifty thousand dollars this morning."

Mac let a low whistle hiss from between his lips as he watched Wilkes open his car door.

"That's a chunk of change."

"The horsemen are worried. Some of them are scared. They've got a lot riding on their animals. They want this maniac caught, and they're willing to pay for it."

Mac nodded to Wilkes and watched him get into his patrol car, fire the engine and drive away.

Thankfully nobody had been killed, although Emma had come closer this morning than he wanted to remember.

He turned for the barn and glanced up in time to see Rahul duck into the Dago stable.

A coincidence, or had he been watching and listening the entire time?

MAC JOLTED AWAKE IN the loft, sat up, pushed back the sleeping bag and turned his head to the right, trying to pinpoint the noise he heard coming from somewhere outside the barn.

Below him in his stall, Navigator paced, his nervous movements putting a measure of warning deep down in Mac's gut.

He pulled on his boots, walked to the ladder and climbed down from the loft, pausing at the base of the rungs to listen again.

Closing his eyes, he tilted his head to the right, picking up a raking noise at the far left corner of the barn.

Animals? Maybe a raccoon looking for a bite, or a skunk who'd wormed his way in under a paddock door.

Navigator put his head over the gate and gave Mac a rumbling nicker as he stepped close and put his hand on the colt's forehead. Horses were extremely sensitive to danger, more so than humans.

"What is it, big guy? What's got you pacing tonight?"

Again, the sound drew his attention to the far end of the barn.

The hair at his nape bristled.

Mac walked over to the tack room door, reached inside and flipped the switch on the motion-activated lights to the off position. The element of surprise would be his tonight.

Moving to the open front entrance, he stepped out into the night. His breath crystallized on the cold air as he moved to the corner of the barn and paused against its rough exterior.

He leaned around the corner for a look and spotted movement through the rows of panel-gated paddocks next to the barn.

The quickest route of attack was back through the stable and out the rear exit.

Backtracking, he slipped inside, pulled his cell phone out of his coat pocket and dialed 911. He whispered the information to the 911 operator and closed the phone.

Hugging the shadows along the stall-lined corridor, he reached the back entrance and silently pulled the pin on the latch.

Easing the door open a crack, he prepared to slide it wide and take down the thug before he could run away this time.

Sucking in a breath, Mac froze, his brain registering the scent that hung on the air outside the barn door.

He tested the smell again to confirm the worst-case scenario playing in his mind. Smoke?

He smelled smoke.

Chapter Nine

Mac's heart hammered a determined rhythm against his ribs. Fire explained Navigator's restless behavior.

He put his eye to the sliver he'd opened in the door and saw movement in the midst of a fiery glow emanating from the outside corner of the barn.

Locking his hand on the pull handle, he forced the door open and lunged for the man holding a lit portable propane torch, and wearing a bandanna over his face.

"You son of a bitch!"

Surprise widened the arsonist's eyes above his disguise.

Mac cocked his arm and rammed his fist into the guy's face before he could move.

He waved the lit torch at him, grazing the front of Mac's coat.

Flames took hold. The stink of burning fabric fumed to Mac's nostrils. He smacked the fire out against his chest and charged, smashing the thug in the face with all the anger he could muster.

The arsonist dropped the torch and stumbled back. Mac kicked the cylinder away from the barn and hit him a third time.

He went down.

An eerie glow pushed away the darkness as Mac stepped out beyond the corner of the barn.

Horror rocked his nerves. He watched flames licking up the outside wall of the barn at two separate ignition points. A high-pitched whinny blasted through the night air. He bolted into action.

Grabbing the thug by the back of the neck, he dragged him to his feet. "Move!" He muscled him around and headed them for the entrance back into the barn.

"No! I'm not going in there, it's on fire." The thug offered resistance Mac didn't have time for. Navigator was his only focus. He had to get him out of the barn, but he also didn't plan on letting the creep get away this time.

"Have it your way." Mac reached up, cupped the back of the thug's head and slammed his forehead into the door jamb, knocking him out cold.

Before the jerk could hit the ground, Mac caught him and flopped him over his shoulder like a sack of grain.

He stepped inside the barn and flipped the light switch. The overhead lights came on, highlighting the belches of smoke invading through the eaves on the side of the stable where the fire was beginning to feed on the siding.

There wasn't much time.

Mac reached Navigator's stall and heaved the thug off his shoulder, flopping him down onto the floor in a heap.

He grabbed the colt's halter and punched in the access code. Nothing.

He punched it in again, feeling the bite of frustration across his nerves. This time the latch responded and he opened the stall gate. He stepped into the cubicle and reached out to the scared horse. His eyes were beginning to sting. The smoke was beginning to make its killer descent from the ceiling to the floor.

The overhead lights flickered and went out, plunging the cavernous death trap into darkness. Only the glow from Emma's outdoor Christmas lights shone into the inky blackness.

"Easy." He put on Navigator's halter in the near dark, snapping the lead rope shank onto the ring at the bottom.

Turning for the stall gate, he saw movement coming at him through the haze, but realization dawned too late.

Wham. Mac's teeth rattled in his head with the bone-jarring blow to his forehead, which had the distinct ring of a metal shovel.

He launched backward.

Hot liquid gushed from his nose.

Clutching the lead rope, he let it slide through his hand until it caught on the knot at the very end. He applied a death grip to it, hanging on for the ride.

Navigator bolted forward and lunged out the open stall gate, taking Mac with him, as he charged over the top of the thug, who dropped the shovel and ran for the door.

"Whoa. Easy." Mac sucked in a lungful of smoke and tried to calm the horse as he dragged himself to his feet and stumbled for the exit, the glow of colored lights growing dimmer with each passing second.

The sound of the door's rollers grinding along their tracks put a measure of panic in his blood.

The gap of light narrowed.

Reaching the door, he pulled it back open, led the horse outside and sucked in a breath of fresh air to clear his lungs.

"Mac!"

He turned and saw Emma on the safe side of the thug she'd pitchforked to the door panel of the barn as he'd tried to lock them inside.

"I called the fire department the minute I smelled smoke. They'll be here any minute."

Relief rocketed through his veins. They were safe now. All of them. "I'll trade you a Kentucky Derby horse for a felon.

One's going to win, and the other is going to spend a lot of time in prison."

"Deal." Emma let go of the pitchfork handle and took Navigator's lead rope from him. She turned and jogged him well away from the barn.

He pulled the tines out of the thug's clothing and grabbed him by the scruff of the neck. Dragging him back a couple of steps, he yanked down the bandanna hiding his identity and found himself staring at a kid, maybe eighteen years old at the most.

"The sheriff's en route. You're going down for three counts of attempted murder and arson."

He fell in step behind Emma and the horse, hearing the hum of sirens echoing across the bluegrass.

"I don't know what the hell you're talking about. I didn't try to kill anybody."

Mac pulled him up short. "What do you call setting the barn on fire with me inside, a cookout? You took potshots at us with a .22 and you sabotaged Firehill's tractor and almost got someone killed this morning. Three counts."

"I didn't touch your damn tractor."

Mac hustled the punk to the side of the house and shoved him down against it into a sitting position where he could detain him until Wilkes got there.

Had he really expected the kid would admit the crimes? Still, he hadn't denied the shooting incident, or setting the fire, the two worst offenses. He'd only bucked over tampering with the John Deere that had nearly gotten Emma killed.

Mac squatted next to the thug and mopped at his own bloody nose.

"How did you do it? Did you use those fancy surveillance cameras you hid in the haylofts to spy on Navigator, learn his routine so you'd know when you could access the barn to poison his feed with bute?"

"You're flipping crazy, man. You know that? I don't know anything about any cameras."

Mac pushed up onto his feet and watched the kid cross his arms over his chest. Concern hedged his thoughts, pushing caution to the forefront of his mind.

Was the kid telling the truth about the tractor incident and the cameras? He didn't appear to be a very sophisticated liar, but Mac needed to be sure. Emma's life could hang in the balance.

"How old are you?"

"Old enough."

"Old enough to be charged as an adult. You're going to do hard time. And a lot harder time if you don't tell me who you work for."

The kid turned green, enhanced by the Christmas bulbs hanging overhead. "Brad Nelson."

"Brad Nelson over at Cramer Stables?"

"Yeah."

Mac relented and took a step back, watching the kid's bravado deflate like a leaky tire as his head bobbed forward into his hands.

He swallowed and glanced up as Emma came toward him from the left and a fire truck pulled down the driveway on his right.

"Did the colt settle down?"

"Yes. I put him in the east paddock, over by Victor's barn, for now. His crew is lined up there watching the action."

He reached over and put his arm around her shoulders, pulling her against him. "How are you holding up?"

"Much better now that everyone's safe. I can replace the barn, but not—" She looked up at him and frowned. "Your nose could be broken. What happened?"

"The kid hit me with a shovel."

"Ouch." Emma stared down at the guy, a kid she knew

she'd seen somewhere before, but she couldn't place him. "He doesn't look so tough right now. Did he tell you who he works for?"

"Brad Nelson at Cramer Stables."

"The farm that received a threatening letter the same day we did?"

"Yeah. If he's telling the truth, Nelson just used the letter as a ploy to draw suspicion away so he could look like a victim while he perpetrated the attacks."

Behind them the fire crew turned on the draft pumps and attacked the fire.

Mac released Emma, backing her up next to the side of the house, careful to stand in between her and the punk, who again buried his face in his hands. Mac only hoped the magnitude of what he'd done made a lasting impression.

Sheriff Wilkes barreled down the drive with his patrol car's lights flashing, followed by another engine and an ambulance. He climbed out of his patrol unit, spotted them next to the house and hurried over. "Dispatch forwarded your call, Mac. Is this the perpetrator?"

"That's him. He says Brad Nelson over at Cramer Stables is behind the attacks."

The kid looked up, and Mac could see the beginnings of a black eye along the upper edge of his right cheekbone.

"On your feet," Wilkes ordered pulling the handcuffs off his belt. "What's your name, son?"

"Craig McFarlane."

"Did Brad Nelson hire you to torch Clareborn's barn?"

"Yes, sir."

Wilkes glanced over at Mac and Emma. "I'll put him in the car and take your statements."

An ounce of closure settled over Emma as she watched Sheriff Wilkes cup the top of the kid's head with his hand and usher him into the back seat of the police car where he couldn't get away. Couldn't cause any more trouble for anyone.

She leaned into Mac, glad when he put his arm around her and pulled her close to his body.

"What's going to happen to the little worm?" she asked.

"If he's a day over eighteen, he'll do real time. Arson is a serious crime. The sheriff will have to find hard evidence to get him for the shooting. If he has the .22 in his possession, attempted murder charges could stick."

"And the runaway tractor? Did he admit to that?"

Worry ground over Mac's nerves. "No. And he claimed he had nothing to do with the surveillance cameras, either."

Emma shivered and he realized she was only wearing a bathrobe.

"Go in the house, get warmed up. I can handle things from here and we'll go in to the station tomorrow if we need to."

He reached down and wiped at a smudge of soot on her cheek with his hand, but only smeared it.

"I'll put on some warm clothes and come back out. We're going to have to do something with the colt. It's too cold tonight to leave him in the paddock without shelter."

Mac released her and watched her disappear around the side of the house. She was right. They couldn't leave the horse out under the stars. The temperature was already dropping like a rock and they'd run the risk of having him take a chill.

A measure of caution sliced through him as he considered their limited options.

Picking out the fire chief in the midst of the crew, he headed for him, intent on getting an assessment of the smoldering barn's condition. If it was too extensively damaged, they had only one recourse tonight, and it didn't sit well in his gut.

They'd have to stall Navigator in Victor Dago's barn.

"No." Emma shook her head and attempted to remain calm, even though her nerves were a jumbled mess. Tension wrapped around every muscle in her body and started to squeeze.

"There has to be someplace else we can house him." She slid her coat sleeve back over her watch and stared at the time: 3:22 a.m. The fire trucks had long since put out the fire and mopped up the scene. Sheriff Wilkes was probably already kicking down Brad Nelson's door to arrest him, and Craig McFarlane was spending his first of many nights in jail.

"Dammit, Mac. You know how I feel about Dago. Just the thought of being in the same place with him gives me the creeps."

"We have to do something, Em. Navigator won't accept this smoky blanket on his back and it's already in the thirties."

Frustration and fatigue weighted heavily on her judgment and she relinquished her argument. "Okay. But tomorrow we have to figure out something else."

"I'll sleep next to his stall gate if it will make you feel better."

She gazed up at him. "We're a pair, aren't we. Me with my scraped-up forehead, and you with a probable broken nose."

"Yeah, well, it was worth it to finally catch the creeps. Wilkes plans to lean hard on McFarlane for a confession. Then maybe we'll learn the full extent of what he did here at Firehill and the other farms in the area."

"And if he still won't confess to sabotaging the John Deere and hiding the cameras?"

"Then we've got a problem, because somebody did." Mac felt his throat tighten and the tension ramped up in his body. "Come on, let's get the colt into Dago's barn, then we'll re-group in the morning."

"Mac. It is morning."

MAC RAISED HIS FIST and rapped his knuckles on the bunk-house door a couple of times. Inside, he heard a loud thump and the door opened.

One of Victor's grooms rubbed his eyes and stared at him as if he had a horn growing out of his forehead.

"I need to talk to Victor."

The man shook his head, turned slightly and rattled off something in Arabic over his shoulder. Another thump, as someone bailed off a bunk bed and tromped across the floor.

An exchange in Arabic between the man and someone behind him, and Mac found himself facing Rahul.

"Can I help you?"

"I apologize for the late hour, Rahul, but I need to talk to Victor. The fire put Navigator out in the cold and we need a stall in the stud barn until we can get a cleanup crew in."

Rahul said something to his buddies over his shoulder, got a reply, then looked at Mac. "His bunk is empty. The last time I saw him he was headed over to the barn to try and calm Dragon's Soul. The sirens set him off. He must still be in there."

"I'll track him down. Thanks." Mac turned around and heard the door close behind him.

The hair on the back of his neck prickled and he swore he saw movement at the edge of the curtained window as he hit the end of the walkway and met Emma where she stood holding on to the colt's lead rope.

"What did he say?"

"Don't know. Victor wasn't there. Rahul said he's in the barn trying to calm Dragon's Soul. The ruckus from the fire riled him up."

"He's overly excitable."

Mac fell in step next to her, unsure why his nerves were

stretched to the point of fatigue. He glanced up at the barn in front of them and the light emanating from inside. The stud facility was half the size of the main barn, housed a dozen highly secure stalls and had been filled with stallions back in his father's day in the industry.

Emma pulled the horse up short. "Let's put him as far away from Dragon's Soul as possible."

He agreed. The two stallions would tangle if given the chance, and one or both of them could get hurt. "We can lock the stall door and use the outside paddock for access. The two of them will never have to cross paths."

"Good plan." Emma approached the first stall on the left, pulled open the sliding door and walked the big horse inside.

Mac stood near the entrance as she inspected the cubicle, cleaned out the automatic watering bucket and turned on the fill valve.

He glanced up and stared down the wide corridor. Where was Victor? The tack room door stood ajar and the light was on. Maybe he'd chosen to stay close to the animals tonight, make sure they all settled after the night's events, but somewhere in the stable, one of the horses paced.

Mac turned his head to the right, listening to the shuffle of the straw bedding under hooves. A low, rumbling nicker drew his attention to the last stall on the right near the tack room.

Dragon's Soul?

The horse had potential. He'd seen it in the colt's eyes, and if he was handled properly, he could be a contender.

"I'll see if I can find Victor, let him know what's going on."

"Thanks," Emma said, looking up at him, a moment of relief softening the tension around her eyes.

His heart squeezed in his chest. It was possible that his

time at Firehill would end in the next couple of days. The investigation into the attacks and the tying up of loose ends was the only thing standing between him and his motto—Get in. Get out. No emotional attachments....

Turning away from her and the colt, he walked to the other side of the wide breezeway and stared into the first stall through the narrow iron bars that surrounded every one of the stud stalls.

A gangly roan filly stood in the corner with her head low and her eyes closed.

Not exactly a Winning Colors, he decided as he studied her conformation. Concern went with him to the next stall, where he sized up a good-looking chestnut gelding with a blaze running down his face to match his four white stockings. He'd get the superstitious, socks-can't-run crowd of horsemen whispering in the bluegrass. He looked as if he could keep stride with the best of 'em.

Dragon's Soul was becoming more agitated, Mac noticed as he moved closer to the colt's stall. His pacing increased, his soft rumbling nicker becoming more frequent and more pleading.

He glanced up, watching the top of the horse's head above the iron-bar partition. The big colt's ears flicked forward, then back, forward and back.

Concern hurried Mac through his perusal of the next three horses in line, none of which looked like racehorses at all.

What the hell was going on in the Dago barn?

Emma removed Navigator's halter and stepped outside the stall. She pulled the door closed on its rollers and tested the latch a couple of times before hanging his tack on the hook and glancing up to find out where Mac had vanished to.

"Emma!"

The urgency in his voice sparked concern as she scanned the empty corridor. He must be in one of the stalls.

"Mac?" She hurried along the breezeway.

"In Dragon's Soul's stall!"

She picked up her pace and braked to a stop in the partially open doorway of the unruly colt's stable.

Her knees threatened to buckle out from underneath her.

"Call an ambulance. He's still breathing."

She dug in her coat pocket and pulled out her cell phone. With shaky hands she punched 911 into the keypad and stared into the cubicle at Victor Dago's bloody body.

He was crumpled in the corner of Dragon's Soul's stall, with his head kicked in.

Chapter Ten

Mac leaned in close to Victor and put his hand on the man's shoulder.

Judging by the distinct shape of a horseshoe partially angled on his forehead and disappearing into his bloody hairline, the mechanism of injury was obvious.

Dragon's Soul must have freaked and kicked Victor when he'd tried to calm the frightened animal.

One blow from a horse's powerful hind leg, if it landed in the right spot, could render a man unconscious, and in the animal's state of fear, he'd kicked and stomped Victor until he went down and couldn't get out of the box.

A low moan rumbled in Victor's throat.

Mac leaned closer.

"Victor, it's Mac Titus. You've been injured by Dragon's Soul. Emma called an ambulance, they'll be here soon. Hang on."

Victor groaned again, louder this time, and a string of garbled words babbled out of his mouth.

Over Mac's right shoulder the horse pawed the straw bedding with his front hoof. The frustrated behavior made Mac as nervous as hell, but he didn't feel threatened. The big colt's manner had projected concern, not out-of-control fear.

"They're on their way, Mac. What can I do to help?" Emma

asked as she closed her cell phone and leaned against the door frame.

"Catch the horse and move him into another stall. EMS can't work with him in here."

"Are you kidding? He just tried to kill someone. I'll go and get Rahul, he knows how to handle Dragon's Soul."

"Yeah." He nodded and watched her pull the door handle and narrow the opening. He didn't blame her for being leery of the big black colt.

Victor reached out and grabbed his wrist, squeezing with an iron grip that felt like desperation.

Startled, Mac leaned closer. "Hang on, Dago. Help's coming."

In the dim light from overhead he watched one of Victor's eyes flick open. The other one was bloody and swollen shut. His unfocused gaze roamed the stall for an instant and settled on Mac.

"Brief…" Victor whispered, his mouth still moving even after the word was released.

Concern pulled Mac closer to Victor. He tilted his head to the right and leaned in, fearing these could be the man's dying words. "What is it, Dago?"

"Case…" He sucked in a labored breath.

"Briefcase?" Mac said the word and Victor's grip on his wrist tightened.

"In a brief—"

Mac heard the pounding of running footsteps in the corridor and the stall door ground open on its rollers.

"In a briefcase? Is that what you're trying to tell me, Victor? What's in a briefcase? Your contact information?" Frustration ground over his nerves as Victor's grip released and a labored exhale hissed from between his lips.

Mac glanced up at Rahul and Emma, who both stood in

the cubicle breathing hard from their frantic race back to the barn.

He reached over and felt for a pulse on Victor's neck. Nothing.

"Do something, Mac! You have to do something," Emma pleaded.

Victor Dago was a lost cause at this point. He was bleeding out from a massive head trauma…but there was always a chance.

"I'll start CPR."

EMMA STOOD GRASPING THE bars of the stable partition staring into the stall, watching Mac take his second trip around Dragon's Soul.

Worry knotted her nerves and she squeezed the iron bars so hard one of her hands cramped. "Be careful, Mac."

"He's not going to hurt me, Em."

"That's what Victor thought, too." She couldn't get the image of his battered condition out of her head; she was just glad he was receiving care in the back of the ambulance and Rahul was with him. They were headed to the hospital, although things looked grim for the man she'd never much liked.

"Look at this cut across his chest." Mac ran his hand along the black horse's neck and glanced up at her. "How'd he get it in that stall? I didn't see anything sharp. It looks superficial."

"I don't know. Maybe Victor did it trying to defend himself."

"Maybe."

She watched as Mac picked up Dragon's feet one after the other to examine the bottoms of his hooves. He tapped on the aluminum-plate racing horseshoes on the sole of each one, then physically tried to manipulate the shoe.

Nervous tension glided over her senses and locked in her body. What had happened tonight to Victor Dago was tragic. The fact that the Firehill stud barn was the scene of the horrific event made her sick to her stomach.

She stared at the magnificent black Thoroughbred, at his calm, wouldn't-hurt-a-horsefly demeanor, and shuddered. "I'm going to head inside, get a couple hours of sleep before I fall over."

"Wait up, I'll walk you to the house, then come back and tend to Dragon's cut." Mac patted the big colt's neck and pulled open the stall door, stepped out and slid it closed, making sure it latched.

Mentally and physically wired, he fell in step next to Emma and headed for the stable exit, taking a quick glance into Navigator's stall as they passed.

The colt was asleep on his feet.

It would be hours before the adrenaline in Mac's system diluted to a tolerable level. Probably about the time Sheriff Wilkes showed up to take a look at the medical-emergency scene as assessed by the EMS staff and rule it a tragic accident. A terrified animal, lashing out at its handler. God knew the fire had riled all of them. It was the perfect catalyst for the event.

Still, a degree of hesitation married with the measure of uncertainty in his mind.

"I want you to take tomorrow off, Mac. Get some rest. It's Sunday and the danger to Navigator has passed with Craig McFarlane's arrest. I'll take care of making a new batch of mash for the colt in the morning."

Mac pulled her to a stop at the barn door. "Emma, it is morning."

She snorted at his silly replay of her joke and flashed him a tired smile that immediately dissolved as he reached for her and pulled her against him.

"It's going to be okay." He felt her body tremble and pulled her tighter against him. "No one ever expects to see a tragedy like this. No one who loves and cares for horses wants to believe they're capable of something this violent. They're good animals, Emma. Dragon's Soul is a good soul."

She pulled back and stared up at him. "How can you say that? He stomped in Victor Dago's head tonight."

"I couldn't find any blood on Dragon's hooves, or the valleys in his horseshoes."

"Are you saying this wasn't an accident?"

"I'm saying when the Sheriff gets here in the morning, I plan to ask him to test them to make sure." His gaze drifted to her lips. Desire rocked his senses. He reached out and brushed her cheek.

She closed her eyes and turned into his palm, but in the end, he only pressed a kiss on her forehead, took her hand and aimed her for the house while dawn broke on the horizon.

EMMA FILLED NAVIGATOR'S bucket with mash and watched him shove his head into it and start grinding.

"You love that smelly stuff, don't you?" She patted his neck. "Enjoy it now, because you're going to be officially weaned next week."

"Talking to a horse? What is he saying?"

She glanced up and saw Mac looking at her through the iron partition, a contemplative grin on his mouth.

"Can I have some more, please?"

"That's what I thought." He stepped to the stall door and slid it open for her.

Coming out into the breezeway, she paused while he slid it closed and put his hands on his hips. "Sheriff Wilkes is here. He's over at the bunkhouse along with Rahul, telling the crew that Victor died last night."

"Oh, no." Her heart sagged in her chest and she stared at

the ground for a moment, then back up into Mac's face. "This is awful. Has he contacted his family?"

"I don't know. Did he ever mention that he had one?"

"Not that I recall, but then, I never took the time to ask." A wave of guilt swamped her resolve. She felt the sting of tears behind her eyelids. "I should have, and I feel bad for their loss. Family is one of the most important things there is. Without them life would be a lonely place."

Mac's features darkened for an instant and she couldn't help but believe there was something he wanted to say at that moment, but instead, his lips pulled into a thin line.

"Wilkes will be in here next to take a look at where it happened. Do you want to hang around?"

"No. I've got another project I'm working on. I don't know if I could stand to listen to a rehash of the gory details."

"I understand."

She gave him a weak smile and headed out of the barn, feeling the caress of his gaze on her back as she took a right turn and headed for his bunkhouse.

If wishes were horses, all beggars would ride....

Mac mulled the old saying as he took his gaze off of her and turned to walk down the row to Dragon's Soul's new stall. The black colt greeted him with a low-rumbling nicker and shuffled to the stall gate, where he put his muzzle against the bars for Mac to pet him.

"Mac," Sheriff Wilkes said, spotting him from the doorway of the barn.

He headed for Wilkes who carried a clipboard in his left hand. "Sheriff."

"Hell of a tragic accident. I'm sorry it had to happen at Firehill." Wilkes stopped in front of him. "Dago's crew says Dragon's Soul has a mean streak. He likes to strike out with his front legs and if he catches you by surprise he'll knock you down. That's probably what happened to Victor Dago."

Mac held his tongue. He'd listened to the horse and he wouldn't believe it until there was solid proof. "The stall's down here." He stopped outside the cubicle, opened the door, and stepped inside. "I found Victor over there." He pointed at the exact spot, staring at the dark, bloodstained straw in the corner.

"He was barely alive when I got to him."

"According to the EMS run sheet, his injury was catastrophic. He died en route to the hospital."

"Damn." Mac's throat tightened.

"What did you do after you found him?"

"I tried to reassure him while Emma dialed 911. He mumbled something that didn't make much sense, and then he stopped breathing. I checked for a pulse, didn't find one, but at Emma's urging, I started CPR even though I knew he was a goner with an open head wound like that."

"What did he say?"

"'Briefcase.' In a 'briefcase.' I figured he was telling me how to contact his family. Maybe he keeps their names and addresses written down in a journal or something he keeps in his briefcase."

"I had his crew round up his personal items for me. And there was a briefcase. I checked for emergency contact information inside, but there wasn't any. His crew claims his family lives in California." Wilkes wrote something down on the report fastened to his clipboard.

"His Kentucky trainer's license and his driver's license were in his wallet, and I collected that from the hospital already."

Mac tried to reconcile Victor's last words with anything that made sense, and came up empty. "Wait. There's something you should know about Victor Dago. I've got a friend in the Lexington bureau of the FBI who conducts the background checks on every trainer's license application. I was concerned that Victor and his crew could be behind the attacks against

Emma's horse, so I contacted him to check out Victor's. His search came back with no record of Dago's paperwork in the Kentucky system."

"His trainer's license is bogus?"

"Looks that way." Mac watched Wilkes frown. "While we're on the subject of bogus, I checked Dragon's Soul's hooves right after EMS transported Dago and I couldn't find any trace of blood. Since Victor's head injury was so severe, I'd expect to find traces of blood on the horse's shoes, if not on the horse."

Mac glanced at the stall walls as they angled into the corner, and moved in for a closer look. "There isn't even spatter where it should be."

Wilkes leaned in to examine the wooden planks, then pulled a small digital camera out of his jacket pocket and snapped a couple of pictures. "I've got a swab kit in my car. Maybe we better take a look. I'll go get it."

The sheriff left the cubicle and Mac followed him out, anxious for a breath of fresh air and a peek at the morning sun. He wasn't sure how much longer he could stay on his feet, and Emma's offer of a day off was sounding better by the second.

Rahul came out of the bunkhouse, followed by one of the grooms, and headed straight for Mac.

"Mr. Titus," he said, stopping several feet back. "I've just spoken with my employer about Victor's tragic death. He has put me in charge of the stable until a new trainer can be hired to assume Victor's duties. We're going to need more space in the barn. He has authorized me to increase the monthly lease rate to Miss Clareborn, if she will immediately remove her horse from our stable."

The hair on the back of Mac's neck bristled. "Your current lease only includes the use of six stalls. Your boss wants to double that?"

"Yes. Two more of our horses are being released from quarantine in Front Royal, Virginia, tomorrow morning. I will be leaving in the next hour to pick them up. We should return late Monday night. If you'll relay the information to Miss Clareborn and let me know when I return, I'll forward the answer to my employer."

"I'll do that." Mac nodded in agreement, crossed his arms and watched Rahul turn and head back toward the bunkhouse, passing Sheriff Wilkes along the way.

Victor's blood was barely dry and Rahul was already taking over, but then someone had to run the stable until they found a suitable trainer. Still, things somehow felt off with Rahul in charge.

"You know what the implications could be if we don't find trace evidence on the horse?" Wilkes asked.

"Yeah. I know." He reached Dragon's Soul's stall and pulled his halter and lead rope off the hook next to the door.

"Victor may have been murdered and this was all staged to look like an accident perpetrated by an aggressor who can't tell us what really happened here last night."

"Suspecting it and proving it are two different things."

"I'll give you that, Sheriff. Dragon's Soul's reputation isn't stellar. He's not a docile pony. Things were crazy here last night with the fire and smoke. I'm sure he could smell it in the barn—add the blare of sirens, and you've got an out-of-control horse. Hell, even Emma was hesitant to get too close to him, but he's not malicious, Sheriff. He makes a perfect scapegoat."

Mac turned the latch, rolled the stall door open and stepped inside.

Dragon's Soul shuffled toward him. He put the halter and lead rope on the colt. "I'll hold him. You know how to pick up his feet don't you?"

"Yeah." Wilkes opened the test kit, bent over and put

it down on the straw. He took out a wrapped swab and opened it.

"What are you doing?"

Mac glanced up at Rahul standing in the doorway. "Sheriff Wilkes needs to check Dragon's hooves for blood."

Wilkes straightened with the swab in his fingertips. "It's procedure. Since this horse is the only witness to what happened in here last night, I'd like to check for blood."

"It's the law that you must obtain a search warrant before you can collect the evidence, unless you have express consent to do so without a warrant from the animal's owner or handler. Am I correct?" Rahul said, glaring at Wilkes.

Unease spread across Mac's nerves like butter on toast.

"That's correct. Because Dragon's Soul is a living, breathing animal and unable to give consent on his own, lack of consent from his owner to collect evidence will require me to get a court-issued warrant to obtain it."

Mac gritted his teeth, watching a smug look of satisfaction materialize on Rahul's face.

"Then as the horse's handler, I give my consent, Sheriff Wilkes. But I must tell you I had Karrif soak Dragon's hooves this morning in a bleach solution to kill fungus before he applied the lanolin. I'm afraid your evidence went out with the bucket of solution." Rahul turned and walked away.

Mac shook his head. "I'm sorry about that, Wilkes."

"He's right. Bleach corrupts blood evidence." Wilkes knelt, put the swab back in the kit and closed it.

"What's this?" He motioned to the razor-thin cut running across Dragon's Soul's chest.

"He got it somehow last night. It's superficial." Mac rubbed his hand along the colt's neck and watched Wilkes examine the injury.

"If I didn't know better, I'd say it came from a knife blade

The edges are clean. No jagged tearing of the skin. Did you look at his stable?"

"I took a cursory look, didn't find anything sharp at that level in the stall. I thought maybe Victor had done it trying to protect himself."

"Why not just get out of the cubicle? If you're on your feet and moving, you'd head for the door," Wilkes said as he did just that and stepped out into the breezeway.

Mac removed the lead rope and followed him out, latched the stall door and turned toward the stable across the way.

"There was no knife in Victor's personal effects. Maybe it's still in there."

"Do we need a warrant?" Mac asked, not relishing another confrontation with Rahul.

"It's Firehill Farm's property. Rahul has no authority to deny a search. A simple verbal consent from Miss Clareborn would do the trick."

"I'll go get her." Mac hustled out of the barn and headed for the main house.

EMMA STARED THROUGH THE partition bars watching Mac methodically search the stall with a pitchfork, spearing and shaking each forkful of straw to see what fell out, as Sheriff Wilkes snapped pictures with a digital camera to document the scene.

They'd already cleared the bloody straw out of the corner where Mac had found Victor, and the amount of blood that had soaked through the bedding and into the floor made her stomach turn.

The tinny ring of metal clattering against the floorboards drew Mac up short, and she moved into the doorway of the stall for a better look.

"I'll be damned," Sheriff Wilkes said, bending closer for a

look at the pocketknife lying on the floor with its blade open. A blade covered in blood.

"The proverbial smoking gun." Mac leaned on the handle of the pitchfork and glanced up at her.

Wilkes took a picture of the knife and slid his camera into his jacket pocket. "We'll see what the crime lab makes of it. There's a lot of blood on it, more than I think could come from the gash across the horse's chest."

Mac agreed, but he held his tongue. What had seemed like a horrific accident six hours ago was slowly beginning to look like murder, and he didn't want to upset Emma right now, even though he was pretty sure she was already beginning to understand the implications.

Wilkes took a rubber glove out of his pocket along with a baggy. He pulled the glove on, squatted next to the knife, picked it up and put it in the bag.

"I'm going to order an autopsy on Victor's body. There are enough unanswered questions in my mind to warrant an investigation."

Mac pulled in a breath and turned for the stall door. Once outside, he leaned the pitchfork against the wall, feeling a measure of tension in his body that wouldn't dissipate. "What can we do to help?"

"Watch yourselves." Wilkes stepped out into the breezeway. "Contact me immediately if you see anything suspicious, or out of the norm. I should have some results by the end of next week."

Concern plagued Emma's features and creased the space between her eyebrows.

Mac stepped closer to her. Reaching out, he rubbed his hand across her back, feeling the tension in her shoulders. The reality that a killer could be roaming freely at the farm didn't exactly thrill him either.

"I was hired to protect Navigator, and with McFarlane's

arrest, the horse is safe now, but I'll stay on as long as Emma needs me."

"It certainly can't hurt. I'll continue to send a unit out this way on a regular basis for the next week or so."

"Thanks, Sheriff." She glanced over at Mac with a look he couldn't quite decipher, a look somewhere between curiosity and relief.

"I finally remembered where I'd seen Craig McFarlane before last night. He was driving the truck that delivered my sweet feed."

"That would explain how the bute got into the feed sacks at so many farms. I'll question him about it." Wilkes pulled off the protective glove inside out and shoved it into his pocket.

"A heads-up. You're both in line to receive equal portions of the reward money for McFarlane's apprehension. With his confession and Brad Nelson's arrest, the case is officially solved. My department will be cutting the checks." Wilkes turned and headed for the exit.

"Twenty-five grand?" Mac asked as he reached for Emma's hand. They fell in step next to Wilkes and left the barn.

"Oh, hell, did I forget to mention the reward doubled?"

"Yes, you did." He wanted to turn his good ear on Wilkes to make sure he'd heard correctly.

"You're each going to receive a check for fifty thousand dollars. You can come in to the department to pick them up on Tuesday afternoon."

Emma's knees buckled.

Mac caught her.

Wilkes grinned and headed for his car.

Chapter Eleven

Using the first rays of dawn to see the damage, Emma stared up at the massive timbers inside the blackened barn and listened to Mac's report.

"The fire chief said there's no structural damage. None of the heavy timbers burned. The siding on the outside can be replaced and the interior can be pressure-washed to remove the smoke damage. I'll put a call out to a cleanup company. We're lucky it didn't ignite in either one of the haylofts or the place would be a total loss."

"We're lucky, all right. Lucky you were here, that you caught McFarlane and that you got Navigator out in time. Did you mean what you said about staying on?" She stared over at him.

"Every word. There are still too many unanswered questions, like who tampered with the tractor and who installed the surveillance cameras. If Sheriff Wilkes proves Victor's death wasn't an accident…" He turned toward her and grasped her upper arms. "I don't plan to leave until I know you're safe."

The physical contact warmed her skin where he touched her and she looked up into his face. "I don't want you to go, Mac. Firehill needs you…I need you." She let her gaze slide to his lips, rocked up onto her tiptoes, closed her eyes and kissed him.

Desire roared through Mac's body, scorching his resistance

in its wake. He locked his arms around her and pulled her against him. Deepening the superficial kiss, he parted her lips with his tongue and explored her sweet mouth.

The smoky smell of the barn intermingled with her scent of vanilla, straw and the outdoors.

She arched against him, a moan sounding deep in her throat.

Every cell in his body burned for satisfaction. She was balm on his soul. The woman he wanted to lead him out of the desert.

Mac broke the kiss and pulled back, warring with his conscience as he did. She shivered in his arms as she buried her face against his neck.

Reaching up, he stroked his fingers through her hair, cupped the back of her head and closed his eyes, breathing her in while he worked to tame his out-of-control response to her. Maybe it was fatigue busting down the barriers, maybe something more, he wasn't sure.

"I have no right to want you this much."

She pushed back and stared up at him, her whiskey-colored eyes bright in the gloom of the cavernous barn. "No right? You have every right, Mac." She reached up and brushed her fingertips along his scarred jaw. "I don't care about this, or that you lost your hearing."

He closed his eyes, clamped his teeth together and fought the overwhelming urge to jerk away. To put a stop to the soul-stripping deprivation her assessment generated in his mind.

"It changes nothing. You're the same person you were before it happened, aren't you? You're honest and good. You protect people…and a horse, and you save lives. You've sacrificed more than the average person ever has and you deserve to be happy."

She was playing fast and loose with his motto, the one he'd always used to define the perimeters of his life.

Get in. Get out. No emotional attachments.

He opened his eyes, reached up and locked his hand on hers. Staring into her face he pulled her hand away, severing the intimate touch. He released her fingers, but his push-back gesture didn't seem to faze her.

A slow smile bowed her sexy, swollen lips and she stepped back. "I'm fixing supper tonight at the house to celebrate the end of the attacks on Navigator's Whim. I'd like you to come. You're the reason he's safe now. Get some rest. I'll see you at seven." She left the barn.

He stared after her. How in the hell was it possible she'd pegged him like that? His identity as a Secret Service agent had evaporated after the shooting and he wasn't sure he'd ever get it back. In fact he was almost certain now that he couldn't.

Mac walked out of the barn, realizing the cavernous black hole in some ways resembled the pit he'd been rolling around in for a long time. Maybe even since he was a kid. He owed it to Emma to level with her. To tell her that Paul Calliway—a bitter man who'd hated Thadeous, and Firehill, and who'd never let that fact go unspoken until the day he died—was his father.

He crossed the open area from the barn to the bunkhouse and considered how she would take the revelation.

Frustration glided over his nerves. Emma was a straight shooter and he hadn't been totally honest with her. He reached the bunkhouse door and remembered that he hadn't had the chance to clean up the chaos inside.

Dead tired, he turned the knob and opened the door.

A whiff of her scent hit him as he sucked in a breath and glanced around the tidy room. She'd found the time to slip away and take care of the mess left by the intruder. His gaze settled on the freshly made bed covered with a bright patchwork quilt.

Stepping inside, he closed the door behind him, feeling a surge of gratitude swell in his chest.

How was it Emma always seemed to know what he needed, even if he didn't?

EMMA PUT THE LAST PLATE into the dishwasher, filled the soap cup and turned it on. She flipped off the kitchen light on her way out and joined her dad and Mac in the living room, where they talked about what distinguished a good horse from a great horse.

"It's one quarter training and three quarters heart, Thadeous. You can condition them equally, but the horse with heart will give you everything he's got, and then some. Look at Seabiscuit, Canonero II, who won the Derby in 1971 from out of nowhere, and Barbaro. Heart wins races."

She settled on the sofa across from Mac, watching his mesmerizing blue eyes glisten with excitement as he talked to her dad about four-legged legends.

"There's no substitute…for good breeding. I never bought a horse…based on heart. You can train them…to run, but you better start…with good lineage."

Mac glanced across at her and grinned, then turned his attention back to her father. She had to believe he was enjoying the conversation, and she found herself wondering where he'd acquired his horse sense. He was so much more than an amateur.

"I'll give you that. An impressive bloodline is a plus to build on, if the horse has heart."

"Dessert, anyone?" Emma asked as she came to her feet. Her dad chuckled and shook his head. "Not tonight…dear. I'm going to…watch my program…in the den."

Mac stood up and reached out.

They clasped hands and shook.

"Come back soon, Mac. That's…the best…time I've had in a while."

"I sure will." Mac watched the old man manipulate the control lever on his wheelchair and purr into the hallway. He liked Thadeous Clareborn. His mind was still sharp and he knew a hell of a lot about horseflesh, had even witnessed some of the greatest strides to glory.

"I made apple pie and there's vanilla ice cream in the freezer. Would you like some?"

"You're spoiling me, Em, but no thanks, I'm still full from supper."

"Maybe later then, after you help me put up the Christmas tree?"

He glanced at the stack of boxes in the corner marked "C-mas decor," and knew he had to put his inner Grinch aside, at least for tonight. He'd helped her cut the tree, it was time to help her decorate it.

"Tell me what to do."

"I'll get the stand set up, then we'll bring in the tree and put it up in front of the window."

Half an hour later, Mac watched Emma wrap the noble fir in miniature colored lights.

Climbing down from the chair next to it, she rummaged in a box and pulled out a star. She held the tree topper out to him."Would you do the honors?"

He took it, feeling a surge of emotion he'd denied all evening. The Clareborn's were a family and their house was a home.

"Just put it on the top?" he asked, feeling like an awkward kid.

"Yes." Emma's throat tightened as she watched Mac stare at the Christmas star they'd been putting on the tree since she was a child. "Hey." She reached out to him and touched his forearm. "You don't have to do it if you don't want to." She met his dark blue gaze and wondered about his hesitation.

"I want to do it." He turned around, stepped up onto the chair and put the star on the top of the tree.

"How's that?"

She gauged the alignment. "A little more to the left, back toward the window. There. Perfect."

Mac stepped down off the chair and tried to relax, tried to enjoy the time alone here with her. It suddenly didn't matter that his early life had been filled with turmoil at this time of year, every year. It was time to let the past settle into oblivion and live in the moment tonight.

"What's next? I'm ready."

They hung the mismatched ornaments one by one, until the tree was covered in them and Emma was smiling like an excited little girl.

His heart squeezed in his chest as he watched her work. This was important to her. This was a joyous time. He sobered. "I need to check on the colt."

"Not yet. You have to partake in a Clareborn family tradition first."

"What's that?"

"A mug of mint hot cocoa, on the front porch in the swing with the tree lights shining through the picture window."

"I'd go for that."

She smiled at him as she hurried into the kitchen and returned ten minutes later with two steaming cups of cocoa. "Would you plug in the tree?"

Working his way around to the back, he found the cord and shoved it into the receptacle. He stepped back and smiled, before meeting Emma's gaze.

"It's beautiful, Mac. Thank you."

"Thank you for straightening up the bunkhouse." He put

on his coat and took the mugs while she pulled her coat on and opened the front door.

"You're welcome. I knew you were exhausted."

He followed her out to the porch swing and waited for her to get settled before he handed her one of the cups. He sat down next to her seeing the lights shimmer through the glass.

"I need to discuss something with you, Emma."

"Discuss?"

"Rahul announced this morning that he has taken Victor's place at the stable."

"I don't have a problem with that."

"He wanted me to tell you they'd like to lease the other six stalls in the barn. His employer will increase the lease amount. The only catch is he wants Navigator removed from the stud barn immediately."

"That's ridiculous. He knows I've got nowhere else to house the colt until the barn is restored."

"I know they're going to need at least two more stalls beginning on Monday night when Rahul returns with the horses from quarantine in Front Royal. He gave you until then to make a decision."

"I've got a check for fifty thousand dollars coming. Maybe I should give Rahul and the sheikh notice to vacate the stud barn. I only leased to them because I was desperate. I'm not desperate anymore."

"I know." A measure of caution attached to his thoughts. Would Rahul find a way to retaliate against her? Or would he leave quietly?

"Has Doc Remington called yet with the results of Navigator's bloodwork?"

"No. He's suppose to let me know in the morning."

"We're going to need to continue the remedy until midweek. He'll probably be clean by then."

"I hope so. Hey, thanks for chatting with my father tonight. He loved it. I haven't seen him that animated in years."

"I enjoyed it, too." Mac drained the last drop of mint cocoa from his mug and pulled in a lungful of crisp night air. This was living. Living like he'd never done before.

"I'll check on the colt before I turn in." He angled to face her, watching the sparkling lights reflect in her eyes.

He reached out and took her chin, easing her to face him. "I've been thinking about the things you said to me in the barn this morning and it reminded me of something else you once said."

"Sounds serious."

"It was at the time. You drew a comparison between my wanting to hear again with my left ear and your hope that Navigator could win the Derby. And I made peace with one of them. I won't ever regain the hearing in my left ear, but your colt can win."

He leaned forward, kissed her on the lips, handed her the empty mug and stood up. "Good night, Emma."

"Good night, Mac." She listened to his boots on the front steps, then watched him until the night wrapped him in its velvety blanket.

Letting down the walls in her mind, she instilled his image and realized she'd fallen for Mac, like a newborn filly on unsteady legs.

She left the swing and went inside the house to rinse out their cups in the kitchen sink and go to bed.

MAC SHOVED HIS HANDS in his coat pockets and headed for the stable. He focused on the light emanating from the barn's doorway, but his thoughts were squarely on Emma as he looked for an opening in the hedge on the perimeter and stepped through it.

The garbled sound of raised voices made him stop to listen.

Turning his head to the right, he tried to decipher exactly where the argument was coming from.

Two of Dago's grooms shuffled into the doorway at the mouth of the breezeway. Notes in Arabic seemed to raise and lower with the hand gestures one of the men made repeatedly.

He didn't know what they were saying, but it alarmed him. He stepped back into the protective cover of the hedge to wait it out. Once they were gone, he'd check on the colt and turn in for his first solid night's sleep in weeks.

Movement at the far left corner of the barn caught his attention. He focused on the exact spot were he'd seen it, trying to pick it out again in the darkness.

A shadow? A person? He couldn't be sure. He didn't see anything until a man in black edged to the front corner of the barn and flattened himself against the wall, twenty feet from the arguing grooms.

Was he listening, too?

Mac held his position, feeling the first tingle of realization take hold in his brain. He'd never considered that someone could be spying on the Dago stable. Did that mean there were cameras planted somewhere in the stud barn, as well?

The two men left the stable, headed for the bunkhouse, still yelling at each other, but Mac kept his eyes on the man dressed all in black.

On his right he heard the bunkhouse door slam. He maintained his focus, determined to track the thug.

The man pushed away from the wall and jogged toward the bunkhouse.

Mac's caution level cranked up. He tried to blend deeper into the brush, going still as the man hurried past his location and up the driveway.

Turning back toward the yard, Mac hugged the hedge, listening to the man's nearly silent footsteps padding along on the asphalt on the other side of the protective barrier.

He reached the main drive.

Mac went down onto his belly in the grass, catching sight of the black-clad figure as the man reached the main driveway leading out of the farm and onto the highway.

The sound of a vehicle drew his attention and he could just make out the shape of a dark-colored van without its headlights on. It stopped on the road.

He heard the unmistakable grind of the van's side door sliding open on its track, and sliding shut a second later. The van accelerated away and the mysterious intruder was gone.

Mac came to his feet, turned and headed for the barn. If his suspicion proved correct, he should be able to find what he was looking for in a matter of minutes.

Hanging close to the bushes, he made his way back to the break in the hedge, jogged across the open space and ducked into the barn door. He slowed and scanned the corridor for any of the grooms. The stable was empty.

The stud barn was half the size of the main barn and only had one hayloft.

Mac stopped at Navigator's stall and glanced in at him through the iron-bar partition. The colt was sacked out on his straw and didn't bother to raise his head.

Focused on the ladder up into the loft, Mac took even strides for it, reached it and climbed up, coming face to face with a stack of hay he couldn't see over.

He pressed against the wall, squeezing through on the right-hand side. Working his way to the end of the stack, he stepped out into a small area next to it, ducking his head to keep from banging it on the low-hanging rafters.

From this vantage point he could see the entire stable and down into each individual stall where the horses slept—where Victor Dago had been attacked.

Mac went to his knees, brushing away the hay on the floorboards as he crawled closer to the edge of the loft. A third of the way across the front he uncovered what he was looking for: a thin piece of black coaxial cable stretched out in the narrow joint. He didn't have to follow it to know where it was going to lead.

The Dago barn, aka Rahul barn now, was under surveillance.

A knot lodged in the pit of his stomach. Whoever was at the other end of the camera must have witnessed Victor's murder, but why in the hell were they spying on Firehill Farm in the first place? What did they want?

"Hey!"

Mac's head jerked up and he found himself staring down into the angry face of one of the grooms he'd seen arguing with another only minutes ago.

"Down!" He motioned wildly.

Mac came to his feet and shook his head, then patted a bale of hay with his hand. "I need to borrow a bale." He pointed down into Navigator's stall and watched the request register with the upset man.

He nodded his approval and stepped back.

Mac knocked a bale down with his booted foot and kicked hay back over the cable he'd just exposed.

The groom snagged the twine ropes and hefted the hay bale down the corridor, where he dropped it next to Navigator's stall door.

Tension knotted Mac's muscles as he squeezed back through the narrow opening and climbed down the ladder.

The man stood across the breezeway, leaning against the wall with his arms crossed, watching Mac with an intense stare he could feel dissecting him as he pulled out his pocketknife and cut the strings on the bale.

Measuring off a flake of hay, he unlatched Navigator's door, slid it open and tossed it into his feeder.

The groom didn't budge.

Mac pulled the stall door closed and tested the latch before turning to face the man. "Hey, thanks." He motioned to the open hay bale.

A nod was all he got from the groom, who remained, arms crossed, against the opposite wall like a sentry guarding some unknown secret.

Mac headed out of the barn, feeling the man's scrutiny on his back with an intensity that set his nerves on edge. Something was going on. Something big.

Something his gut told him could harm Emma if he didn't rout it out.

EMMA PULLED THE PLUG on the Christmas tree lights and walked down the hallway to the den, thinking about Mac.

The sound of the TV told her that she'd find her dad asleep in his wheelchair with the set still on. It had become a nightly routine to wake him, turn off the tube and lock up.

"Dad," she said as she entered the room and headed over to close the curtains. "It's 10:30."

"Emma. Come here...I want to...show you something."

She pulled the cord, closed the drapes and stepped over to where he sat in his wheelchair holding a framed picture in his hand.

"I wasn't certain...but tonight confirmed...my suspicions."

Concern jumbled her nerves as she knelt next to her dad. "Suspicions? About what?"

"About who." He angled the photo toward her and she clutched the other side of the frame to steady it. "Look...at this." He tapped his finger on the glass covering a shot of a horse she recognized standing in the winner's circle.

"It's Smooth Sailing at the Clark Handicap in Louisville."

Her dad nodded and tapped the glass again with more vigor than before. "Him… Look."

Emma took the frame from his hand, moved to the lamp on the end table and stared down at the picture. "Who is he?" she asked.

"Paul…Calliway."

"No way. The infamous Paul Calliway trained Smooth Sailing?"

"Owned…him. Won the race… I claimed him…from. He swore…he would destroy Firehill someday."

She studied the photo staring at the tall man. He held Smooth Sailing's reins close to the bit, and wore a tweed jacket and a familiar-looking fedora. The same fedora she'd seen hanging on a nail in the tack room from the time she was a little girl. The dusty old felt hat that Mac had taken to wearing until his haircut.

Mac.

Reality clawed into her senses as she picked out the familiar features on the little boy standing next to Paul Calliway, wearing a mile-wide grin on his face.

She looked up at her father, feeling her throat squeeze shut and her eyes begin to water. "Mac Titus is Paul Calliway's son?"

"And Firehill's…enemy."

Chapter Twelve

Emma rolled over in bed for the umpteenth time and finally sat up. She reached over, turned on the lamp and picked up the 8x10 framed photo from off the bedside table.

How could he? How could Mac lie to her? The details of her dad's long, drawn-out story of perceived betrayal and Paul Calliway's promise of vengeance someday had kept her from falling asleep at all.

Was it possible that Mac could also be here at his father's bidding? And what about his last name being different? Did that prove intentional deception so he wouldn't be discovered?

She rubbed her finger across the image of the little boy's sweet face, staring at his happy smile. There was only one person who could tell her what was going on inside his head that day, and now.

Sliding the picture onto the table, she threw back the covers, climbed out of bed and pulled on her robe.

It was two in the morning, but she didn't give a damn. He'd shattered her trust. She wanted the truth.

Emma picked up the framed evidence and headed for the bunkhouse.

THREE LOUD KNOCKS ERODED Mac's sleep and dragged him into semi-awareness.

He rolled over when he heard three more and sat up, staring at the bedside digital clock: 2:11 a.m.

A jolt of concern fired through him as he turned on the lamp. Maybe there was trouble in the barn? Worried, he threw back the covers, stood up and pulled the extra blanket off the foot of the bed.

"Coming," he hollered, wrapping it around his naked lower half. He went to the door and pulled it open.

Emma stood on the step in her robe, muck boots and no coat.

"Emma? What are you doing here? Is the colt okay?"

She stared at him long and hard, too long, too hard, before she slipped past him into the room. "The horse is fine, but we need to talk, Mac."

He closed the door and turned around, watching her move to the small café table in the corner, place a picture frame down on it and rub her hands together to warm them.

"It's cold tonight," she whispered, drawing his attention to the firm round protrusion of her nipples pressed against the silky fabric of her robe.

He tried not to stare, but his mouth went desert-dry and he scanned the room for his jeans, spotting them hanging over the back of one of the stools at the table.

"I'll get dressed and you can tell me what's on your mind, Em."

"Please don't call me that." Her eyes were watery in the light coming from the lamp. He stepped toward her, watching a shiver rock her body.

"Have I done something to upset you?" He stopped an arm's length away, catching his first glance of the photo inside the frame she'd placed on the table.

His chest tightened. The jig was up. He reached for his jeans, pulled them off the back of the chair and headed for the bathroom door.

Emma watched him walk away and stared at the hard, lean line of muscles tapering down his back and ending below the level of the blanket. She sucked in a deep breath. He better take a shirt, too, or she'd think of nothing else but wanting to smooth her hands over him.

Arming herself for battle, she picked up the frame and held it like a shield until he exited the bathroom and moved into the kitchen. "Would you like something to drink?"

"No thanks. This won't take long."

He pulled a bottle of orange juice out of the fridge, set it on the counter and turned to face her.

Emma swallowed, trying not to gape at his ripped abs and the trail of dark hair that disappeared into his jeans below his belly button. "My dad showed me this tonight, after he saw you at dinner." Her voice cracked. She cleared her throat and pulled her shoulders back. "Why, Mac? I trusted you. Why didn't you tell me you were Paul Calliway's son?"

Mac's heart squeezed inside his chest. "Because I knew something like this would happen. Nothing but trouble ever followed him around."

"You know he swore he'd take vengeance on Firehill?"

"Hell, yes, I listened to every plan he ever hatched to get back at Thadeous for claiming Smooth Sailing at that race." He gestured to the frame in her hand and stepped closer, close enough to take it from her and study the picture.

"This horse was my dad's one true shot, Emma. After he lost him, he was never the same, not that he was much good before that. Christmas Eve of that year he drank himself to death. I couldn't get him to leave the tavern that night. He died of alcohol poisoning outside in his pickup."

Mac put the picture down on the table and looked into Emma's eyes. They glistened with tears she was working to blink back, but she was failing miserably.

"I carried his poison around for a long time before I realized he was a bitter man, and I had to let it go. It didn't belong to me, Em." His throat constricted, tingling with emotion. "You know I'd never do anything to hurt you, or this farm. Hell, it feels more like a home than any place I've ever been."

A tear escaped and slid down her cheek.

He reached out and smoothed it away, determined to end her mistrust and empty his soul so he could give voice to the emotions stirring inside of him now.

"Say something Emma. Ask me to leave, ask me to stay, but say something."

"You changed your name?"

"My mom remarried five years after my dad died. I took my stepfather's name to avoid the stigma of being Paul Calliway's kid, but it looks like there's no escaping it anymore."

"Your secret's safe with me," Emma said, stepping toward him, grateful when he put his arms around her and pulled her against his bare chest.

She let go of all her doubts and breathed him in, feeling the heat level come up in her body along with a desire she was helpless to resist. She arched against him and heard a sharp intake of breath whistle through his teeth.

"You should go now," he whispered against her ear.

She closed her eyes and stroked her hand across his back, across the firm bulge of muscle under taut skin.

She'd used that line on every man who'd ever tried to coax her into bed, right before she sent them down the road. But she didn't want to go tonight. She wanted to stay. She wanted him.

Emma leaned back and stared up at Mac, watching his nostrils flare as his breathing ticked up. Pushing up onto her tiptoes, she brushed his lips with hers, satisfied when he responded by clasping her head in his hands and forcing his fingers into her hair.

Mac deepened the heated kiss, parting her lips with his

tongue. Touching. Tasting. He broke the kiss and stared down into her upturned face. Instinctually he knew the time to stop was long gone. They'd taken each other to the edge.

Her cheeks were heated, her nipples fully aroused and puckering the fabric of her robe. He wanted to step on the gas, he wanted to hit the brakes. He wanted to pleasure her until she screamed.

"Don't stop, Mac." She brushed her hand across his chest, working her way down his belly, where she stopped at the button on his jeans.

"You don't understand. There's no going back if we start this dance, Emma."

"I don't want to go back, I want you to make love to me before I keel over on the spot." She licked her lips, driving his libido off a cliff.

Inching her fingers lower, over his crotch, her eyes widened when she came in contact with the bulge underneath. He watched her swallow hard and a slow seductive smile blossomed on her sexy mouth.

His need increased to the point of pain. He reached for the tie on her robe and pulled the bow loose. "Are you sure, Em? Say the word and I'll stop."

"Go." She tilted her head to the side, exposing the slender column of her neck to him. Desire burned through him. He worked to slow his movements as he smoothed the robe off of her shoulders, down her arms and onto the floor.

He brushed his hands from her narrow waist down over her bottom, and caught the hem of her short nightgown, pulling it up and over her head.

Emma fidgeted under his hot blue stare, her body superheating to white-hot.

"You're beautiful, Em." He reached out and brushed his hand along her cheek.

She turned into his palm and pressed a kiss into it.

"Are you certain?"

She nodded, listening to the whisper of his jeans as he shed them and took her by the hand. Two steps and he was lowering her onto the cool sheets.

Closing her eyes, she mentally followed the tantalizing sweep of his hand as he explored her body. Touching where no man had touched. She tensed, then relented as he pulled one of her nipples into his mouth and teased it with his tongue.

She arched against him, reached up and cupped the back of his head, driving him hard against her as she fought to control the need rocking every nerve ending in her body.

Mac toyed with her nipples, enjoying the sweet rumble of frustration in her throat akin to a growl. Smoothing his hand down her flat stomach, he worked his finger inside of her.

She gasped, a sweet, sharp intake of breath that jacked his need into high gear.

The time for titillation was over, she was ready and so was he. He raised up and stared down into her face as he parted her legs with his knee.

A flash of terror zipped across her features and vanished a second later into a tentative smile.

"What is it?" he asked, concern cooling the tension in his body for an instant.

"I've never been with anyone, Mac. I want you to be the first."

The air locked in his lungs as he gazed down into her face. Leaning down, he trailed a path of kisses along her shoulder. "We'll go slow, then," he whispered.

Emma closed her eyes, put her trust in the man she'd fallen for and gave herself to him.

"WHAT THE HELL?" Agent Conner said, staring at the only monitor in the surveillance van streaming a live feed.

Agent Donahue swiveled the captain's chair at the front

of the van and stood up. He'd just relieved Agent Walker and wasn't up to speed yet.

He climbed into the back and studied the monitor, watching the situation shape up in front of him. "This can't be good."

Three men congregated in the stud barn corridor and began what looked like a search of some sort.

"Did Agent Ryan happen to get a listen tonight?"

"Yeah. He heard an argument between Karif and Javas. His translation is on the notepad lying on the seat in back."

Donahue spotted it and eased past Agent Ryan's chair in the narrow confines of the aisle. Plopping down on the bench seat, he picked up the legal pad and studied the conversation, looking for information that would get them one step closer to finding out what the terrorist cell was planning.

Sheik Abadar is scheduled to arrive at Keeneland racecourse the afternoon of the 24th, just prior to the race. Dragon's Soul will run.

Curse words here. They're missing a horse. Without nine horses they can't win?

Karif is angry because Victor didn't file the proper paperwork to get the horse shipped from Dubai to Front Royal. He may be stuck in the port in New Orleans. It's a long trip.

Karif warns Javas to keep an eye on Miss Clareborn and her groom. He doesn't trust them, and he'll kill them if necessary.

What the hell were they planning, Renn wondered? All the satellite phone chatter rumbling out of Firehill had dried up in the last week. They weren't using computers or regular phone lines.

There had to be more than just a discussion about a horse race on Christmas Eve—that didn't present an actionable threat. And what about Mac Titus and Emma Clareborn? He'd always been suspicious of Mac's role at Firehill because of his Secret Service connection to Abadar, but that suspicious link had evaporated the night Victor was murdered. Mac Titus was in the clear and quite possibly their best hope.

Renn gritted his teeth and pulled in a deep breath.

"You better have a look at this, Renn," Agent Conner said over his shoulder, as he adjusted the camera lens. "They're onto us."

"Dammit." He watched Karif's ugly face enlarge in the monitor just before the screen went black. "It's too dangerous now to reinstall it. Maybe it's time to consider plan B."

Frustrated, he turned and headed for the front seat of the van and his secure cell connection to the director of the National Security Agency in Maryland.

MAC PRESSED THE BUTTON on the stopwatch as the colt breezed past his spot on the rail and thundered down the front stretch.

"Good news," Emma said from next to him. "Doc Remington says Navigator's bute number is down to twenty-three percent and that was from the blood taken on Friday. He's going to be clean before the Holiday Classic."

Mac reached out and put his arm around her, pulling her up next to him in the crisp chill of the morning after.

"That's great." He watched the colt lay into the first turn. "I've got my own good news."

"Oh, yeah? Spill it."

"The tow-truck driver and a mechanic will be here at noon to rescue the John Deere and get it fixed. And the cleanup company is getting started on the barn this morning. They said it should take them about four days to restore it, less if we clean all of the tack ourselves."

"That's the best news. Only four more days in the stud barn."

He felt her shudder and took his eyes off the colt moving down the backstretch. "You feeling it, too?"

"Like sand in my teeth."

"They were watching every move I made this morning getting the colt ready to run. I also found a camera in the loft of the stud barn last night."

She looked over at him. "Same kind as you found in our barn?"

"Yeah."

Navigator galloped into the clubhouse turn and barreled down the homestretch, blitzing in front of him. He stopped the clock and turned to Emma.

"I want you to steer clear of the stud barn. If you do need to go in there, don't go alone. Find me first."

"I'm not helpless, Mac. I wield a mean pitchfork."

Caution congealed in his veins. He reached down and raised her face to his. "Something is going on in that barn, and I'm worried about your safety. Someone in that crew may have tampered with the tractor. Which means they could try again. Promise me you'll do what I'm asking." He pinned her with his stare, hoping she'd accept his warning and stay clear until he could get more answers.

"Yeah. Okay. If you feel that strongly about it, I won't venture over there without you."

A measure of relief looped around his nerves. He leaned in and kissed her, feeling a wave of desire rush through his body.

Every exquisite detail of making love to her last night was forever seared in his brain. "Did you talk to your father?"

"Yes, this morning. It took some doing, but I convinced him you weren't here to destroy Firehill Farm by Paul Calliway proxy."

He chuckled, even though it was gratitude grinding around inside his head and not humor.

"We'll cool the colt and get started on the mash. By Friday we should be able to go back to regular feed."

"Thank goodness." She snagged the lead rope. "I'm tired of smelling like cabbage. If I had any free-range chickens, they'd have pecked me to death by now." Grinning, she walked out onto the track to where Grady Stevens stopped Navigator and bailed off the sweaty colt.

Taking a hard look to his right, Mac spotted Karif and two other men from Dago's crew, watching them from farther down the rail.

Caution churned in his gut and melded to every nerve ending in his body. He didn't trust them, he didn't want them anywhere near Emma and he planned to give his concerns full rein until he got answers.

He glanced back at her standing next to Grady, a smile on her sweet lips as she sucked up the details of the morning's gallop and Navigator's progress.

His heart squeezed in his chest. For the first time in his life, he'd made a real emotional connection.

EMMA WORKED ON THE NEW makeshift cutting board she and Mac had erected on some hay bales in front of the bunkhouse. The feed barrel was half-full now, and she put down the butcher knife to give her hand a break.

Mac put his down too and wiped his hands on a towel lying on the board. "I'll make us some fresh coffee. Come in and get warmed up."

She met his sultry stare with one of her own. He'd either read her mind, or he was as revved up as she was right now.

"Sounds like a plan. My hands are freezing." She looked up at the sky, noting the thin veil of flat, white clouds that had settled over the bluegrass. She could see her breath in the cold air and she hoped like crazy it didn't snow, at least not until after the running of the Holiday Classic.

Following Mac, she stepped inside the warm bunkhouse and closed the door on the world outside.

Together they slipped off their coats and she trailed him into the kitchen. Leaning against the counter, she watched him pour water into the hopper on the coffeemaker, measure a couple scoops of grounds into the filter and turn it on.

She moved up behind him, wrapped her arms around him and pressed her face to his back, feeling his body heat warm her frozen cheek. "Oh, you feel good."

Mac rubbed his hand across hers where they crisscrossed his chest. Heat fired through his body. He turned in her arms and locked his around her, picking her up off of the floor.

She wrapped her legs around him as he found her lips and carried her to the edge of the bed. Slowly he lowered her onto the quilt and eased his body in between her legs. "Are you warm yet?"

"Blazing," she whispered, her lips inches from his right ear. She shivered beneath him as he moved the lip-assault down the side of her neck in incremental degrees, each one more heated than the last. She moved against him, and he reached for the button on her jeans, popped it out of its loop and slid the zipper down.

Ecstasy was two minutes away.

EMMA COULD STILL FEEL the heat in her cheeks an hour later. She finished chopping the last bag of carrots, scraped them off into a bucket and dumped them into the barrel Mac was mixing.

The crunch of gravel under tires brought her gaze up to the driveway, and she saw Sheriff Wilkes jockey his patrol car into a parking spot and kill the engine.

"I hope he's got news about Victor," Mac said, continuing

to work the carrots into the mix with his bare hands. "The longer the unanswered questions persist, the less likely we'll know what really happened."

An unsettled sensation glided over her nerves. She tried to make something out of Mac's reasoning, but she couldn't. If it turned out Victor had been murdered, and not by a horse, then his killer was still at large.

"Sheriff." Mac nodded. "Any news on Victor?"

"I'll tell you, it's the damndest thing. I contacted the coroner's office this morning to put in a request that an autopsy be conducted and they claimed his body was picked up almost before it arrived at the morgue."

"A family member?" Vibes of caution shot into his brain.

"Not if last names have to match. The clerk on staff says he was claimed by a man who signed the name R. Donahue. Don't know who he is, but I'm sending a deputy over there now to investigate. If we can't find him, any physical evidence goes out the window."

"Any luck locating his next of kin?"

"Dead end all the way around, and the phony trainer's license doesn't give us a paper trail to follow. His driver's license was a fake, too. I'm here to ask a few more questions of his crew."

"If Arabic isn't your second language, you'll have to wait until Rahul gets back tonight. He's in Front Royal and he's the only one who speaks good English."

"Thanks for the heads-up. I'll come back tomorrow."

Mac went back to stirring the mash.

"I'll keep you posted." Wilkes tipped his hat to Emma and headed for his car.

"That's too weird." Emma watched Wilkes drive away. She turned to Mac and put her hands on her hips. "Bodies don't just take off, unless someone doesn't want anyone to know anything about Victor Dago. Which reminds me, Rahul, the new kingpin of the stable, wants a decision tonight, and he's bringing in more horses?"

"Yeah. Two."

"I think I'm going to give him two weeks' notice to vacate the stud barn. That will give them time to run Dragon's Soul in the Holiday Classic before they have to clear out."

She stared at Mac, who appeared to be daydreaming or something. "Mac, did you hear me?"

"Yes. I heard you. Sounds like a good idea, but these guys are cagey. Will you let me handle Rahul?"

"He's all yours. I'm going to go in and get washed up, then fix something to eat. Wanna come?"

"You go ahead, I'll clean up out here, give the colt his three-o'clock feeding and see you in half an hour."

Emma headed for the house. No cabbage today; instead, she smelled like carrot.

MAC WIPED THE MASH off his hand and arm and pulled his cell phone out of his coat pocket with sticky fingers. Em was right, bodies didn't just walk off with mysterious strangers. Maybe the key to all the clandestine activity on the farm was somehow tied to Victor Dago—dead or alive he was still causing a stir.

He punched in Doug Cahill's number at the FBI. It rang four times before rolling over to voice mail. "Hey, Doug, it's Mac. Can you do me a favor and recheck that name in the California racing commission's database? Mr. Dago has relatives out there and they may have a record on his background check. Thanks."

Closing his phone, he dropped it into his pocket and glanced across the paddock.

The sooner Rahul and his crew cleared out of the stud barn the better. The restoration company was making progress on the main barn, and by week's end they could move the colt back into his old stall. Things would return to normal.

Snagging the feed bucket by the handle, he walked to the barrel and scooped it full of mash.

When he spotted two men, one on either side of the barn doorway, tension diced the muscles across his shoulder blades into confetti, but he gritted his teeth and walked across the paddock.

Caution bristled the hairs on the back of his neck as he approached the entrance, sizing up the level of resistance he could see in the set of their shoulders, in the way they tracked his every movement with cold black stares and simultaneously stepped together in front of him to block the entrance. From inside the stable, Karif hollered a string of Arabic at them and they stepped aside.

He walked between them and into the breezeway. It was intimidation, pure and simple. Another reason for Emma to steer clear of the stud barn.

Deep in the corridor he spotted Karif with a pencil and notepad in hand. Karif glanced up at Mac, then went back to whatever he was doing.

Mac reached the colt's stall, turned the latch, slid the door and stepped inside. He closed it part of the way while he hung the feed bucket and stroked the horse's neck, listening to the rhythmatic sound of a voice coming from one of the stalls. "Thah-mahn-ee-ah...thah-lath-ah...sit-ah...sub-ah... wa-Had...ar-bah."

Counting?

He didn't know a word of Arabic, but he knew counting when he heard it.

Mac patted the colt's shoulder, slipped out of the door, rolled it closed and moved down the breezeway, pausing only long enough to get a good look at what was going on before he walked out of the barn past the sentries, and headed for the house.

Karif was writing down a series of numbers in neat little rows on the paper, numbers Javas was reading off from the inside lip of each horse in the stable.

It wasn't unusual to find a number tattooed there; every Thoroughbred had one for identification purposes.

But not every horse in their stable was a Thoroughbred, so why did they need a tattoo at all?

Chapter Thirteen

Emma saw the truck's lights through the picture window as the vehicle turned into the driveway and pulled down into Firehill. It broke right onto the road leading to the stud barn. "Looks like Rahul is back from Front Royal with their horses."

Mac rolled his glass between his palms and sat forward on the sofa. "I'll head down there right now."

"You could do it in the morning."

"And miss getting a look at their new additions? Has it struck you as unusual that three of the horses in their stable aren't even Thoroughbreds?"

"Yes. But I just assumed they were companion animals for the other horses, there to keep them calm."

"I saw Karif writing down numbers that Javas was reading from inside the horses' lower lips. All of them."

"Now that's weird." She stared across at him and watched a muscle flex along his jaw. "Maybe two weeks is too long."

He met her gaze. "Maybe. But it's fair."

"Can I see you later?" she asked, stepping closer to him, feeling the first measure of awakening spread over her body.

"Sooner if you'd like." He flashed her a seductive smile, touched her cheek, handed her his empty glass and left.

MAC PULLED HIS COAT OFF a peg by the back door, and stepped out into the night, sensing the dropping temperature as the air hit his face. Every light in the stud barn was on and the squeak of horse-trailer gates and the crunching of hooves on gravel piqued his interest. He knew something was transpiring in the stable, but he didn't know what. Drug trafficking, maybe? The thugs dressed in black could be DEA, ATF or FBI.

Walking across the yard, he toyed with any additional acronyms he could think of, but in the end he was certain the goings-on couldn't be good for Firehill, and they had the potential to devastate Emma.

He would never let that happen. He'd developed a fondness for the farm and the farmer's daughter.

Pushing through the hedge, he stepped out into the open and walked the fifty feet to the barn.

His cell phone vibrated in his pocket. He stopped next to the entrance to answer it.

"Hello."

"Mac. Doug here. Sorry to just be getting back to you, but I've had a hell of a time tracking down that information and hanging on to it."

"What have you got?"

"I found Victor Dago in the California database."

Mac patted his pocket, trying to find his pen and pad. "Let me get something to write the information on."

"I don't think you need to worry about that. Victor Dago is dead."

"I know he's dead. He died the day before yesterday."

Silence reached across the line for what seemed longer than necessary. "Doug?"

"According to the California records, Victor Dago died two years ago, Mac."

Caution worked through him. "You said something about trying to hang on to the information?"

"Yeah. I'd no more than accessed it when someone wiped the file. Watch yourself. This has government op written all over it."

"Thanks, I'll do that. Take care." He closed his phone and shoved it in his pocket, staring into the heart of the stable, where Rahul led a rangy-looking horse into the stall next to Navigator and slid the door shut.

Whatever they were hiding could be behind the southeast gate on the farm. Drugs, guns or any other contraband that could be smuggled into the country. Maybe the racehorse business was just a front for their operation. And if the real and the fictitious Victor Dago were both dead, then who was the man he'd tried to save?

Rahul looked up about the time Mac stepped into the barn. He immediately headed toward him, and met him midcorridor. "Mr. Titus, I see your horse is still in our stable, and I hope you're here with Miss Clareborn's answer."

"As a matter of fact, I am. The main barn is being restored right now and we'll move the colt out of here on Thursday or Friday."

Rahul nodded. "Good. Then she has agreed to our terms?"

"Miss Clareborn has authorized me to give you and your employer two weeks' notice. You can vacate the barn immediately after the Holiday Classic."

He studied Rahul for his reaction, half expecting anger, but a smug smile developed on the man's mouth for an instant before his features changed up, and his brows pulled together. "I understand. Please tell her we will comply with her wishes, but I'm afraid there won't be any stables left in two weeks' time."

"Sounds like a business problem for you and your employer

to solve. Maybe you'll have to purchase your own farm. Good night." Mac turned around and headed for the exit, taking a quick look at the colt before he left the stud barn.

Granted, they were going to have a difficult time finding a stable willing to lease to them with their reputation in the bluegrass, but two weeks from now Rahul and his crew wouldn't be Emma or Firehill Farm's problem anymore.

He sucked in a deep breath, trying to reconcile the foreboding looping around in his head as he crossed the open area and headed for the bunkhouse with Rahul's last words stuck on rewind.

No stables left in two weeks' time? What the hell did that mean? Someone would let them in.

EMMA PULLED BACK THE covers and slipped into bed next to Mac. She spooned herself against his naked backside, letting the skin-on-skin connection infuse her with his body heat.

"Um, you're cold," he said.

"I won't be for long." She brushed her hand over his hipbone, and reached into dangerous territory, feeling his growing need in the palm of her hand.

He growled and rolled over, pulling her on top of him. "You're a bad girl, Miss Clareborn, sneaking out of the house after dark for a secret rendezvous."

"Sneaking out is easy. I used to do it all the time as a teenager when my dad would forbid me from galloping a rank horse in daylight. It may as well have been an open challenge to mount up and take the horse around the track in the dark instead."

"This ride is different, Em." He reached up and smoothed her hair behind her ears, sending a tingle through her body that resonated down to her toes.

"It's a lot more complicated," he whispered.

"Not really." She put her hands on his chest and pushed up onto her knees.

Mac groaned as she lowered herself onto him and started to move.

Waves of pleasure hammered her body and she gave herself over to the timeless rhythm, focused on the escalating excitement that teased her closer to ecstasy with each thrust, until she maxed out on top of him and climaxed seconds before he did.

Satiated, she collapsed onto his heaving chest and closed her eyes, listening to the thump of his heart under her ear.

She was in love with him. She knew it at that moment, felt it in her bones. But she didn't form the words, or speak them. Mac wasn't a horse, and like he said, this ride was more complicated than any she'd ever taken on a Thoroughbred in the middle of the night.

MAC HELD ON TO EMMA long after she'd fallen asleep on his chest. He stroked her silky hair with his fingers in the darkness and warred with his growing feelings for her.

Working alongside her, touching her, making love to her all played hell with his motto, turning it into a sham statement he wasn't sure he could accept anymore.

But she deserved so much better than a battle-scarred bodyguard who had nothing to give her.

He rolled her gently off him and onto the bed, tucking her body in next to his as tightly as he could. He closed his eyes and fell asleep with the scent of her hair in his nose and a knot in his throat.

By morning she was gone.

MAC FLIPPED ON his blinker and turned onto New Zion road, then took a left onto the Newtown Pike for the ten-mile trip into Lexington. He glanced over at Emma, who stared out the passenger-side window of his pickup and hadn't said two words since they left the farm.

Heck, she should be jumping up and down on the seat next to him right now, excited about collecting her reward money. It would go a long way toward preserving her dream. Instead her sullen mood was beginning to rub off on him.

"What's up, Em? This is the answer to Firehill's dollar issues, at least in the interim between now and the Derby in May. I'll give you my half if it will help."

She turned around and looked at him. "No way. It's yours, you earned it, and you're right. I'm happy that the financial pressure is off for a while. And when Navigator's Whim takes the Triple Crown, I can put him out to stud. Things couldn't be more sound." She turned back toward the window. Mac focused on the road in front of him, content with silence for the moment.

Emma blinked hard, working to keep from tearing up. In ten days Mac would leave. In ten short days her life would resume without him in it. Maybe she should tell him how she felt about him, maybe she should say the words to him…I love you…dammit.

He'd just leave sooner.

She'd felt the hesitation in his touch last night. Heard the regret in his voice when he said it was complicated. Well, he got that right.

Straightening in the seat, she raised her chin. She'd survived without him before she hired him, she'd survive without him once he was gone. But her heart wouldn't.

"The station is on East Main Street," she said in a voice barely above a whisper. She cleared her throat and mustered her resolve. "Do you know how to get to it?"

"Yeah. I take heartache lane, a left on I'm-no-damn-good and stop at you'll-end-up-in-misery." He looked over at her and grinned.

She grinned back, but she wasn't buying it for a second.

MAC LOOKED ACROSS the desk at Sheriff Wilkes and felt his muscles pull tight. "What are you trying to say?"

"You've got to leave this Victor Dago thing alone." Wilkes thumbed the stack of paperwork on his desk and didn't look up for a second. "I've been advised to rule Victor Dago's death an accident and close the case. No more questions, no more digging around." He leaned back in his chair.

"I guess it doesn't matter then that I found out the real Victor Dago died in California two years ago, not in that stall at Firehill," Mac said.

Emma reached out and squeezed his arm. "When did this happen?"

"Last night. My buddy with the FBI called just before I gave Rahul your two weeks' notice to move out of the stud barn."

"Let it go, Mac." Wilkes shook his head. "Pursuing it will only end up rocking the boat and pitching someone into the water."

He tried to relax, but he couldn't. He was more convinced than ever that something big was going on at the farm. That someone on Dago's crew had murdered him and staged it to look like an accident. And that whatever they were hiding was somewhere behind the southeast gate of the farm.

Wilkes pulled open his desk drawer. "Here they are. Don't spend them all in one place." He handed Emma hers, then Mac his.

Emma stared at the check for a long time to make sure the ink was dry, then glanced over at Mac, who was already folding his and stuffing it into his wallet. "Thanks, Wilkes. I'm just glad everyone's horses are finally safe."

"Yeah, thanks," she said as she pushed back her chair and stood up.

Mac reached across the desk, shook Wilkes' hand and they left the office.

Emma didn't speak until they reached the pickup and he'd unlocked the doors.

"Can you take me by Central Bank on West Vine?"

"Sure." He fired the engine and pulled out of the parking lot.

"You should have told me about Victor."

"I didn't want you to worry. Besides, we were too busy last night to talk about it."

Her insides went to mush, and she had to force herself to scrub the sexy images from her brain. "Tell me you're going to take Wilkes's warning and steer clear of Rahul, his crew and more questions."

He didn't answer, raising her worry level. "Mac!"

"I can't, Em. Something is going on in that barn, something illegal, and they were willing to kill to shut it up. It could have a tremendous impact on the farm. And you. I've got one last thing to check out before I quit."

She didn't like the sound of that, but he had a point. Why would anyone not investigate and let someone else get away with murder? It didn't make sense.

Mac flipped on his blinker then turned in to the drive-up teller lane at the bank. "I want to know what Rahul was doing that day out at the southeast gate."

"There's nothing out there but unstable limestone caverns."

"Exactly." He pulled the plastic vacuum cylinder out of its holder and waited while she filled out the deposit slip she'd taken out of her pocketbook. "It's the perfect place to hide. No one from the farm goes down there, and they operate with impunity. If I can find out what they're up to, I'll contact one of my buddies with the Bureau and we'll clean them out."

She handed him the check and deposit slip. He slid them into the cylinder, closed it and put it in its cradle, then pushed the button. It sucked up the tube and disappeared.

"What do you think? A drug ring?"

"I don't know," he said.

A minute later, the cylinder dropped. Mac extracted her deposit receipt, handed it to her and pulled through the lane.

"It's five o'clock and I'm starving. Want some supper?" he asked.

"Yeah. Let's splurge, we're loaded right now."

"You've got it, babe."

"Then I'm going Christmas shopping."

MAC STOOD AT THE track rail watching Navigator blaze the backstretch and lay into the clubhouse turn. He looked down at the stopwatch in his hand and smiled. If Navigator stayed on this pace, he would best his fastest time of 1:53. By half a second.

He glanced up as the colt crossed the line and stopped the clock: 1:52 and 2/5.

"I'll be damned."

"Morning," Emma said, walking up beside him to take a spot on the rail.

His throat tightened. He looked sideways at her. "How'd you sleep?"

"Like a baby, after I wrapped all the presents I bought last night and stuffed them under the tree."

"Good thing we had a pickup to haul them home in."

She reached out and put her hand on his, then turned it over to reveal the stopwatch he held.

"Holy cow, he's so fast." She smiled big and he focused on her lips, watching her smile fade like frost on the bluegrass with the morning sun bearing down.

Disappointment beat a path through his body and trampled his heart. She hadn't come to him last night. Hadn't pulled back the covers and slipped in beside him.

Part of him was grateful. He'd compromised her and taken

her virginity, but the other part of him ached for the feel of her body tangled up with his.

The sound of raised voices redirected his attention. He looked over the top of her head to the stud barn, where Rahul and Karif were arguing, Karif with his hands up in an I-don't-know position, and Rahul with his on his hips. "I wish I knew what they were saying," he reasoned. "Then maybe I'd have a better chance of figuring out what they're up to."

"In a week or so it won't matter, Mac. They'll be gone, and so will you."

He stared down at her, reached out and brushed her cheek with his fingers.

She closed her eyes for an instant, reached up and pushed his hand away.

"Emma," he said, feeling a knot twist in his chest. "Wait."

"Save it, Mac. I'm a big girl, I know how this ends." She grabbed the lead rope off the post and walked out onto the track to meet horse and rider.

Mac sucked in a breath and pushed back, turning for the hot-walker and a stack of towels to wipe down the colt. He was glad she knew how it ended, because he sure as hell didn't know anymore.

EMMA FOLLOWED MAC AND Navigator into the stable and down the corridor, noticing that Dragon's Soul was once again housed in the stall where Victor had been found, and two more horses had been brought into the barn, one on either side of Navigator's cubicle.

A chill skittered over her skin and raised goose bumps on her arms inside of her coat sleeves. How had she allowed this to happen? How had she agreed to let someone like Victor Dago, or whoever he was, lease her barn. In that instant she vowed never to let desperation override her gut instincts again.

"Miss Clareborn."

She looked up and saw Rahul step out of the tack room door and walk toward her.

"Yes." Walking slightly past the colt's stall, she stayed close to where Mac slid the gate open and led him inside.

"I would like a definite time of when you'll be moving your horse out of our stable?"

The gooseflesh came back as she studied Rahul, who stood much too close to her at the moment. "Mac."

She was relieved when she heard the stall door roll closed, and felt him at her left side.

"The smoke damage is just about cleaned up. We'll have him out of here on Friday morning after his gallop," Mac said as he reached out and clasped her elbow.

She relaxed, feeling her caution level drop.

"Good, but now that I've added two more horses, and I have one who was shipped into the port at New Orleans and must be picked up, I'm afraid you will have to wait until my employer arrives next week, to receive payment."

"That's not a problem. Is the sheikh coming to watch Dragon's Soul run in the Holiday Classic?"

"Yes. He'll be here the afternoon of the twenty-fourth."

"I look forward to meeting him."

Rahul nodded. "If you'll excuse me, I must hitch the horse trailer to the truck and go."

"Drive safely." She turned around with Mac and walked out of the barn. Worry clung to her thoughts and she couldn't hold it in any longer. It spilled out by the time they reached the back door of the house.

"You're going out to the east gate right now, aren't you?" She stared up at Mac, searching his face for a confirmation and felt the first wave of fear glide over her nerves.

"Yeah. Rahul is leaving, the timing couldn't be better and I may not get another chance. Mind if I ride Oliver?"

"You can't go out there alone, Mac."

"I'm a big boy with a gun, Emma."

"You better saddle Dandy too, then, because I'm coming with you no matter how big your gun is."

Chapter Fourteen

Mac pulled the cinch tight and clamped his teeth together as he stared across the saddle seat to where Emma adjusted the stirrup leathers, then mounted Dandy.

"I can handle this, Em. You don't need to go."

"I'm sure you can. That's not in dispute. But I'm not going to let you go out there alone. We don't have a clue what's beyond that gate."

She had a point, some spunk and too much common sense, for a woman who rocked his mental and physical world the way she did.

He took his loaded backpack off the saddle horn, put it on, clasped the reins and turned the horse for the paddock gate leading into the pasture.

Who was he kidding? She had more at stake in this than he did. Still, he'd packed an extra clip of ammunition for his pistol in case they met with armed resistance. He was a bodyguard, whether for her or her horse, and he still had an obligation to protect them both.

Emma rode through the open gate. Mac closed it and mounted Oliver. Emma took a cautious look in the direction of the stud barn, and didn't see any of the crew around.

"They all headed in for lunch at noon," Mac said, adjusting the old hat on his head. The hat that had belonged to his father.

She'd realized it the moment she'd seen it on Paul Calliway in the picture her father had shown her. He must know it, too.

"Let's get while the getting is good." He spurred Oliver into a trot.

She eased in next to him on Dandy, posting as they rode parallel to the fence, over a rise and out of sight of the stud barn. Relaxing, she reined her horse down into a fast walk, then tried to enjoy the feel of cool air on her cheeks and in her lungs, the sun on her head and the man riding next to her.

"Want to know the story behind that hat?" She glanced at him.

"Sure."

"I guess the evening your dad delivered Smooth Sailing to Firehill, he and my father got into a terrible fight. It seems they each owned equal shares in the horse. Fifteen thousand dollars apiece, that's what they'd paid for him at the Keeneland sale, because even though he had a worthy pedigree, his legs weren't entirely straight, and he didn't have much speed."

"I remember," Mac said, staring straight ahead.

"My dad asked Paul not to put him in the claim race, but he did it anyway, and when he claimed the horse, he ended up owning Smooth Sailing."

"What's that got to do with this dusty old hat?"

"Paul got into his pickup and drove away, but as a parting shot, my dad said he pulled off that hat and flung it into the field out front."

"In other words, he threw in the hat." The fuzzy memory took shape inside his mind, somehow adding a degree of clarity to his childhood that hadn't been there before.

"Come on." Feeling the need to break out, Mac spurred Oliver into a gallop and turned him wide for a back-way approach to the grove of pines, in case any of the crew happened to have followed, or saw them leave the paddock.

The cool air spit icy needles against his face and made him

feel alive inside, even as the old hat on his head reminded him he had a past beyond his total recall.

Paul Calliway hadn't been all bad, or all good. He'd been human.

Emma slowed Dandy on the top of the rise, then reined him to a stop next to Mac and Oliver. "Do you think they know we're here?"

"No." Mac dismounted. "But keep your eyes and ears open."

"Let's put the horses in the center of the trees. There's plenty of grass in there for them to graze on while we're gone, and they can't be spotted from the road."

"Did you bring the hobbles?" he asked.

"Yeah." She took the reins and picked a path into the spiral jungle, weaving between trees, listening to the hollow thud of Dandy's hooves against the earth.

This spot had always been her sanctuary, and now it was a place to hide? Her only consolation was that Mac was here with her, and she didn't have to protect Firehill alone as long as he stayed.

She broke out of the grove and moved into the center, where she opened her saddlebag and pulled out two sets of leg hobbles. She handed a set to Mac and put a set on her horse, then removed his bridle so he could graze uninhibited. She hung it on the saddle horn, and watched Mac do the same.

"Let's try to stay in the tree line as much as possible. If we see any of them, take cover or hit the deck."

A rush of excitement roared through her as she fell in step behind him. He picked a path in between the pines and stopped in the same spot where they'd first spotted Rahul.

Mac went to his knees, then pulled off his backpack. Rummaging inside, he found his mini field glasses. He raised them to his eyes and dialed in a clear view of the southeast gate.

Scanning back and forth, he surveyed the line of trees just beyond the gate and saw nothing.

Still, he couldn't deflect the blade of caution that sliced across his nerves. He lowered the binoculars. "You should stay with the horses, Emma. Let me do this alone."

"No way. I'm safer with you, Mac. Besides, they'd be in a vehicle or on foot, and we'd spot them well before they ever reached us."

There was that stroke of common sense he loved.

Damn.

"Come on. Stay low." He slung the pack onto his shoulder and moved forward, careful never to leave cover as they worked a path to the fence and pulled in next to a clump of brush.

The sun was almost directly overhead, but it warred with the chilly afternoon air and left him feeling cold. Staring into the dense patch of trees behind the gate, he thought he saw something move.

He put his finger to his lips and pointed to the spot.

Emma's heart threatened to jump out of her chest as she stared into the thicket, listening to the crack of branches as someone, or something, moved closer to their position.

She watched Mac retrieve the field glasses and raise them to his eyes, lower them and grin.

He handed them to her. She stared through the lenses at a deer picking its way through the underbrush toward the creek.

"Cute." She handed the binoculars back to Mac, fighting an overwhelming feeling of relief. She wasn't cut out to be a spy. She preferred to get her excitement from a fast horse on an oval patch of turf, or from the man next to her.

"Come on. We'll cross the fence here and make our way to the road. If they're coming in and out of here all the time, we should be able to pick up a trail that leads us straight to their operation."

Mac stretched the wire for her to crawl through, then she held it while he did the same. Once on the other side, he took her hand and moved them out into the open.

Tension zapped his senses, putting him on full alert. Glancing back and forth, he watched for threats, and stopped when they reached the closed and padlocked gate.

"Your dad put this on?"

"Yeah. He wanted to make sure no one could drive a rig in here. It's too dangerous."

Searching the hard-packed earth, he spotted the outline of a boot print and followed it, working his way along the narrow overgrown road that disappeared into the trees less than seventy-five feet ahead.

The hairs on the back of his neck bristled as he took Emma's hand and pulled her along, scanning the thickening foliage as he moved forward. They were sitting ducks out here. Prime targets if Rahul's crew showed up shooting.

Mac picked up the pace, pushing into a jog, aiming for cover as the road narrowed and funneled down into a single path.

"There it is," Emma pointed. "That's the cavern my dad dynamited closed years ago."

Mac stared at the narrow opening at the base of a rising hill that sloped away from the creek. "It's not closed anymore."

Caution jolted through him as he studied the path in front of them for confirmation and found it in the well-worn vegetation leading straight to the mouth of the cavern. "Do you remember anything about it?"

"I'm the reason he blasted it. My friends and I would ride our horses out here to hang out. He was afraid someone would get hurt if it collapsed in on its own, so he helped it along. It's so deep we never found the bottom."

Emma shuddered, remembering the first time she'd ventured into the cave and stirred up a swarm of bats. "It's large once you're through the small opening, then back for about fifty feet. Past that it begins to narrow until you're on your knees crawling along. We didn't explore beyond that point. Too creepy."

"The odds are Rahul and his crew like to walk upright, too, so if their operation is inside, it'll be close to the opening." Fear shattered her nerves as she watched him unzip his backpack, pull out a flashlight, hoist it back onto his shoulder and unholster his pistol.

"Stay close."

She wouldn't have it any other way, she decided as she followed him to the opening of the cavern with her hand on his back.

Mac prepared for a full-on assault, turned on his flashlight and charged into the cavern.

"Damn," he said as he shined the beam of light around the space. "If they ever had anything set up in here, they've cleared it out." He focused on the multiple sets of footprints pressed into the loose soil on the floor and tracked them with the beam, watching the cave narrow just like Emma said it would.

Straining to hear, he tried to focus as he moved deeper inside, but the place was empty.

They were gone and any proof of their operation had gone with them.

"Look!" Emma stepped past him and hurried deeper into the cavern. "There's something back here."

Mac reached out to stop her. To warn her he wanted to check it out first, that it might not be safe.

He lunged forward.

The flashlight tipped down in his hand. The beam shimmered across a copper-colored wire, but it was already too late.

Emma tripped on it with her foot.

The tiny click of a detonator pinged on his eardrum. It came from behind him.

Booby-trapped.

He dived for her.

All hell broke loose as the cave mouth closed with a deep rumble he felt in his bones.

Emma sucked in a mouth full of dust as Mac body-slammed her from behind and knocked her into the dirt.

Pure darkness swallowed her up, but she came up fighting, scratching and clawing at the cave floor to get up off of her belly.

Where was Mac? Where was the light? Where was the air?

She choked and tried to cough out the dust.

Reaching beside her, she touched the cold hard wall of the cavern. Using it to get her bearings, she pulled up onto her knees and sat back on her butt.

"Mac!" she yelled, coughing and choking on the dirt and debris in the air, working to make her eyes focus in the blackness while her stomach churned.

An explosion?

They'd been shut in the cavern by an explosion.

Terror clutched her throat. She fought to maintain her composure. She had to find Mac.

He'd knocked her forward into the tunnel to protect her. He must be closer to the opening. She went onto all fours, crawling forward, shoveling back the dirt with her hands as she moved.

"Mac! Where are you? Can you hear me? Please hear me," she whispered, feeling the first streak of panic glide over her nerves.

A moan followed by a deep inhale and coughing turned her attention back the way she'd come.

At least she thought it was the way she'd come, but the depth of the black hole had turned her perception on end.

"Emma! I'm over here." The sound of his voice clarified it. She pivoted at the same time the flashlight beam bit into the darkness, blinding her for an instant before her eyes adjusted.

The percussion from the blast must have propelled him right past her.

"Are you okay?" She crawled toward him, her heart racing in her chest.

"Nothing's broken, but my leg's hung up."

Fear strained her emotions and she wondered if she was going to die in this hole along with the man she loved.

Shuffling to a stop beside him, she put her hand on his back. "Give me the flashlight." Reaching out, she took it out of his hand and shined the beam along his legs until she found the problem. A couple of large rocks had landed during the blast, and caught the outside seam of his jeans below the knee. Another inch and they would have crushed his leg.

"I can't get enough sideways leverage to pull it loose."

She put the light down and grabbed Mac's leg above and below where his pants were caught. "On three, we'll pull. One. Two. Three."

Emma tugged, but nothing happened. She exerted effort again, still nothing. "Damn. You're going to have to slip out of your pants to get them loose."

"For you? Anything. But it's not going to be easy. Can you pull off my boot?"

Moving in behind him, she grabbed his cowboy boot in both hands and pulled it off.

Mac felt like a two-year-old tangled up on the jungle gym

as he lay on his belly, fighting to unsnap and unzip his jeans. He finally accomplished the task, then took a breather.

"You're going to have to pull my other boot and hold on to the other side so I can crawl out of them."

"Okay." She snagged his other boot and pulled it off, then pulled the hem of his right cuff.

Mac crawled forward with his arms and felt his feet clear the hems of his jeans. In less than two seconds he was free and climbing to his feet.

Emma picked up the flashlight and spotted him in it, shining it up and down his thighs. "Ooh. Look what I found. A just-about-naked caveman."

Mac snorted, more to clear his lungs than to acknowledge her silly joke, but right now a sense of humor was all they had going for them.

Reaching down he gently pulled the light from her hand, turned and shined it on the wall of rock and soil the explosion had dislodged and deposited in the mouth of the cavern.

They were in serious trouble. No one knew where they were. He estimated there was at least five feet of debris between them and daylight.

"Dammit, I'm sorry, Em. I never should have let you come out here with me. I should have forced you to say home."

She came to her feet then picked her way through the rubble to his side. "You did this to protect me, and Firehill, and because it's right."

"Yeah, well, if we live through it, we can debate. Right now, we've got to find a way out of here." Desperation hitched to his nerves as he scanned the cavern, searching for something besides their bare hands to dig away the soil.

"What was it you thought you saw back there?" He pointed the light deeper into the cave.

"Something, equipment maybe, I only caught a glimpse before the explosion."

"Let me go first this time."

"Sure, but you'll need these." She reached down and took hold of his jeans and started to pull. A moment later, Mac joined her and they yanked until the fabric gave, and ripped away, sending them both back on their feet.

"Another inch and that would have been your leg, and then what would I have done?" Emma sobered, letting the reality sink in. She sucked in a raspy breath and handed him his pants with one leg shredded below the knee. "I'll find your boots."

Glad for the momentary distraction, she spotted his boots lying side by side in the dirt, picked them up, emptied them and straightened, watching him pull on his pants. Her cheeks went hot watching him button up.

"Thanks," Mac said taking the cowboy boots from her and pulling them on. "I've got some water in my backpack. It'll wash down the dirt."

He reached out for her and took her in his arms. "We're going to dig out of here."

Cupping her head against his chest, he held her close, then released her. "Come on, let's have a look at what you think you saw back here." He aimed the beam of light into the cavern, picking a path forward, then stopped to snag his pack and his pistol from out of the dirt.

Ten feet farther in he found what she'd seen, what had pushed her across the trip wire and possibly sealed their fate.

"It's a satellite phone." Mac went to his knees and turned over the bulky gray metal box. He popped the latch and flipped the cover open. Inside was a handset and a dial pad. "Hold this." He handed the flashlight to Emma. She focused the beam on the box.

Mac picked up the receiver then pressed the on button. Nothing. He pressed it again. Nothing.

"This is what Rahul has been doing out here? He's been using this satellite phone to talk to someone?"

"Overkill. Why not just use a cell phone or a landline?"

"I don't know. But the signals from these can be encrypted. If you didn't want anyone to know what you were talking about, this is the way to go."

"An encrypted phone to talk about race strategy with the sheikh?"

"I doubt it was anything that innocuous." Caution fired into his brain, but he put his concerns aside for the time being. They had to get out of this cavern before it became their final resting place.

"I've got my cell phone, will it work in here?" She was already pulling it out of her coat pocket. She flipped it open and lowered it into the light. "No signal."

Mac pulled his pack off of his shoulder, opened it and took out the bottle of water. He handed it to her. "Take a drink, but let's be conservative, make it last for as long as we can."

She took the bottle while he dug his knife out of his pocket. He turned the box over, pulled a blade open and worked the screws out on the top and bottom. He separated the sheet-metal cover from the electronics inside and stared at the spot where the phone's battery should have been.

"Here's why it's not working. Someone removed the power supply. It's doubtful that we'd be able to get a signal from underground, anyway."

He tossed the phone's guts aside, stood up and raised the three-sided box into the flashlight's beam. "From a phone to a satellite-shovel."

Mac turned his effort on the mountain of debris and started to dig.

EMMA GLANCED AT HER WATCH—8:30 p.m. on the dot.

"Give up the shovel, Mac. It's my turn." For seven hours

straight they'd been at it, trading off with the makeshift scoop every half hour, scratching into the dirt and rock separating them from the outside world—and from life itself if they couldn't break through.

Mac rocked back from his position near the top of the heap and shuffled down the mound, raising a cloud of dust.

"We're making progress." He took the half-empty water bottle from her, uncapped it and took a single swallow. "Maybe by tomorrow we can open a fist-size hole at the top. Enough to get a cell-phone call out."

"I hope so, but the water isn't going to last that long and the granola bar is almost gone. It'll be harder to work without something to eat or drink."

She stared at the sheen of sweat coating his bare chest, at the ripple of six-pack abs flexed just beneath his skin, and prayed he would save the last of his energy to make love to her again, one more time before they died.

Averting her gaze, she willed the silly thought away and gave in to the sting of tears burning behind her eyelids. She wasn't a girly-girl, had never worried about a broken nail, or a miss-sprung curl, things that set some women off in a panic. She hated to admit it right now to herself, but for the first time in her life, she was scared to death.

"Em?" He reached for her, pulling her against him. "We're going to make it out of here. If it's the last thing I do, I'll push you through the opening I'm going to dig at the top."

The visual on that one struck her as funny. She busted out laughing, pushed back and stared up into his face.

"I can see you doing that for me. That's why I'm in love with you, Mac. You're a man of your word." There, she'd finally put words to the feelings in her heart. The emotion that had taken her by surprise was finally out in the open air between them and it had a name.

Love.

"You don't have to reciprocate. I'm okay with that, but I wanted you to know, just in case…."

Frustrated, she pulled the satellite-shovel out of his hand and headed for the mountain of dirt, feeling a zing of liberation pulse through her veins. She could die now with no regrets.

Mac's heart squeezed in his chest as he watched her go, hearing the echo of her admission over and over in his brain. It was desperation talking, her last hurrah in the belly of a cavern he hoped would release them, but he couldn't be certain that it would.

"Emma, wait." He stepped toward her and paused, uncertain of the clunking sound he could hear. The sluice of shovels scooping into loose earth, and the deep rumble of rocks rolling away.

She stood frozen at the base of the mound.

"Did you hear that?" Mac asked, wanting to be certain.

"Yes. It sounds like people are digging their way in."

Louder, it was growing louder, and closer with each passing second.

Caution spurred him to action.

He unholstered his weapon and reached for her, easing her in behind him before training the flashlight beam and the gun barrel at the top of the mound, where a pinpoint of light began to appear.

Chapter Fifteen

Emma watched shovels full of earth cascade down the mound and held her breath.

Who was on the other side?

Fear skittered through her as she worked the answer. Dago's ex-crew were the only ones who'd been out here.

"Don't shoot," someone yelled through the opening. "I'm coming to you."

English. Thank God. It couldn't be anyone from the stud barn.

She watched in horror as a man dressed from head to toe in black slithered though the narrow opening and rolled down to the cavern floor, then slowly came to his feet with his hands raised. "We'd have come for you sooner, but we needed to wait for dark in case the cavern's being watched."

Mac stepped back, pushing her behind him, with his weapon aimed at the man's center of mass. "Take off the ski mask," he demanded.

The man in black grabbed the top of the mask and pulled it off of his head to expose his face.

Mac sized up the details in a matter of seconds. Clean shaven, military-style buzz cut, straight-faced defiance.

"Who are you?" A measure of caution circulated in his blood, and until he was certain the man wasn't a threat, he'd hold the bead.

"Agent Renn Donahue, NSA. We need to talk, Mr. Titus."

"I'm listening." He lowered the .44 Magnum slowly and holstered it, glancing at another man who wormed through the opening and down the mound, where he pulled two water bottles out of his pack and handed one to each of them.

"Thanks," Mac said, eyeing them both.

"We were monitoring this site up until a week ago when they stopped transmitting from it."

"Victor Dago and his crew?"

"Just his crew, Mac. Victor Dago was Agent Victor Coronado."

Mac's stomach knotted. "National Security Agency?"

"Department of Homeland Security."

The pieces of the puzzle started to slot into place for him, and he guzzled back half the water bottle before he recapped it and stared at Donahue. "You're the man who signed his body out of the morgue in Lexington?"

"Yeah. He was my friend. He's got a wife and three kids in Louisville."

"I'm sorry, man. I found your camera in the stud barn, you must know which one of the crew members killed him."

"Karif. It was Karif and Javas. They smashed his head in with a tire iron and threw him into Dragon's Soul's stall to make it look like an accident."

"Sick bastards. Why don't you go after them for murder?"

"Because we don't know what the cell is planning yet. If we close in on them now, they'll simply scatter and perpetrate the act somewhere else."

"The cell?" Caution roared into Mac's bloodstream, raising the hairs on the back of his neck. "Terrorists?"

"We've been tracking them and their chatter for the last

two months, but all they seem to talk about now are horses, and winning on December 24 at the Holiday Classic."

Mac's gut fisted as more pieces of the puzzle locked into place. "What's your next move? How are you going to stop them?"

Agent Donahue glanced over at his buddy for a second, then back at Mac. The exchange fired up the tension in his body.

"We'd like you to take over where Agent Coronado left off."

Emma's stomach revolted. She reached out and grabbed Mac's arm. "Tell him no! Tell him you won't do it." She swallowed and stepped forward, putting herself between the two men. "You can't. You can't guarantee that they won't kill him, too. Can you?"

She saw the agent's hard-edged stare soften.

"No, Miss Clareborn. I can't. But we don't have time to get another agent in without risking the entire operation. They'd make him the second he stepped foot on Firehill Farm. Mac is already a fixture there and all we'd ask is that he keep his eyes open for any hint of what they've got planned."

Her mind relented, but her heart never would. "Then I guess it's his decision to make." She stepped away and hurried deeper into the cavern where she lost it, and vomited up the water she'd guzzled too much of, too fast.

Mac stared after her, feeling his insides harden as he considered the options, or lack thereof. "Rahul said something strange a couple days ago when I gave him Emma's notice to vacate the stud barn after the Classic."

"What did he say?"

"He said, there wouldn't be any stables left in two weeks' time. I just assumed he meant they'd have nowhere to go, and no one would lease to them."

Donahue blanched and glanced over at his buddy.

Mac turned and walked back to Emma, pulled his handkerchief out of his pocket, wet it from his water bottle and handed it to her.

"Thanks." A sad, sweet smile bowed her mouth. He reached out and smoothed his fingers across her cheek.

"Donahue is right. Rahul and his boys would eat a new undercover for breakfast. It'll be business as usual at the farm, but I'll stay vigilant, Em. I promise."

She nodded and pressed the handkerchief to her mouth.

He returned to stare at Donahue, sensing there was more, something he was withholding.

"I wasn't sure about you, Titus, when you first showed up at the farm, but I watched you fight to save Victor and I knew you were trustworthy. Rahul's contact in the Middle East is Sheikh Ahmed Abadar."

Now Mac wanted to puke, but he locked it down and resisted the urge to stroke his hand over the vicious scar on his left jawbone, the one he'd received when a gunman tried to shoot Sheikh Abadar at point-blank range while on his way to a secret high-level meeting in Louisville with someone from the Pentagon.

Had he saved a terrorist's life?

Mac gritted his teeth and nodded to Agent Donahue. "I'm all in."

"Good, now let's get the hell out of here."

MAC STOOD AT THE RAIL, tracking the big bay colt with his eyes as he galloped at an easy pace and leaned into the first turn for his second lap of the morning.

Tension sent a shiver through his body that he couldn't fight off, and he wished like crazy it was excitement vibrating inside of him instead of foreboding.

The Holiday Classic's race process started tomorrow afternoon in Lexington, and he planned to drive Emma in to enter the colt and pay the twenty-five-thousand-dollar entry fee. Four days later Navigator's Whim would go to the post. Doc Remington had taken a final blood test, and ruled him bute-free. The colt was cleared to run.

They were back in the main stable and away from the stud barn, and he'd seen Emma smiling again. That alone meant more to him than all the rest combined.

But it played hard on his mind that she'd started to come to him again every night since their rescue from the cavern by Agent Donahue.

A measure of guilt sliced though him. He'd welcomed her and hadn't pushed her away again. He'd let their lovemaking grow into a sweet, desperate attempt to hold on to one another and push back the uncertainty.

She'd become his only solace in a gathering darkness he could feel in his bones.

The sound of boots on frost-hardened earth caught his attention and he turned to watch her approach with two cups of steaming hot coffee.

He pulled the leather glove off his right hand and took the mug she offered him.

Together they turned back to the rail.

"How's he doing this morning?" Emma asked, stepping as close to him as she possibly could.

"Grady is taking him around nice and easy."

"Good. I'd hate to have him strained this close to race day."

"You've done a great job, Em. You've done everything right for that horse, and you've got his heart. He'd go to the wall for you if you asked him to."

"Are you the same guy who stood here almost a month ago and said he's just a horse?"

"Yeah, well, he's not just any horse. He's your horse."

Why did she feel as if they weren't even talking about the

same thing? She let the thought pass and took a sip of her coffee. "Rahul is supposed to return midmorning with another horse. Number nine."

"I'll keep an eye out and snoop around when he gets here."

She rested her cup on the rail with her right hand and touched his forearm with her left. "Be careful. Promise me you'll get out of there if you feel like there's anything hinky going on."

"Promise, but you know Donahue is watching this place like a hawk."

"I do, and that's what scares me. He watched Victor die and didn't intervene. Do you think he'd help you? Remember it only takes a second to die."

"Relax, Emma. I know the risks and I've taken precautions."

But she couldn't, and she didn't. "Will you come and spend Christmas Eve with us after the Classic?" Grasping for a thread of normalcy beyond the horse race and anything the terrorists had planned, she hoped he'd accept her invitation without any preconceptions.

"I guess that means I need to do a little shopping in Lexington tomorrow afternoon."

She glanced over at him as the first rays of sunlight crested the hill behind the track and warmed her from the inside out.

"My dad says he's working on a big surprise for me. He's going to reveal it on Christmas Eve—he said he can't wrap it." Excitement pulsed through her. "Our family tradition is to open one present on Christmas Eve. Do you have a tradition?"

"Yeah, my mom and I would always string popcorn. I can still remember the smell in the kitchen, and the needle holes in my fingers."

"We can do that if you want to."

He stared over at her, his dark blue eyes narrowing in contemplation. "I'd like that."

Her heart fluttered in her chest. She watched him drain the coffee in his cup, hand it to her, snag the lead rope from the post and stroll out onto the track to meet Grady and the colt.

He took a hold of Navigator's reins below the bit.

Grady hopped down, and Mac turned back toward Emma, meeting her gaze straight on with a devil-may-care grin that quickly turned to one of raw sexual hunger.

Mind reader.

Heat surged in her veins. She let a brazen gaze slip to his jeans below his belt. Upping the ante, she eyed the length of his thighs. Places she'd touched and explored uninhibited. She knew every inch of him with her eyes closed. The man had turned her nights into a refuge from the coming storm and she ached for him when the sun went down. She ached for him now.

Her throat closed with pent-up emotion she knew she couldn't hide if he continued to target her with his stare.

Shaking her head, she pushed off the rail and headed for the barn. There was tack to clean and Firehill racing silks to size for Grady before the race, but there was also the agonizing knowledge that it could all end any second. And if the terrorists plotting in the stud barn across the paddock had their way, it would.

MAC RUBBED HIS HANDS DOWN Navigator's left front leg below the knee and down to the fetlock joint, feeling for any heat in the ligaments and tendons, before he poured liniment into his palm and rubbed it in with a downward stroke. "He's doing great. No heat whatsoever in any of his legs."

"Let's wrap him up and grab some lunch."

"Okay." Mac picked up the roll of thick cotton bandage, put it against the colt's lower leg and started to wrap from the outside in, finishing just above his fetlock. He pulled a pre-cut strip of cotton tape off his pants leg and secured the end of the wrap to hold it in place. "That should keep him warm and comfortable."

He stood up and glanced out the barn door as the truck, trailer and Rahul rumbled past the stable and drove to the stud barn, where he angled the horse trailer in and stopped.

"He's back."

Emma's nerves thinned to the point of snapping. "Go. I'll put the colt away and play backup for you."

"You'd do that?" he asked, staring at her with a serious glint in his eye and an amused smile on his lips. It was a confusing mix of messages she didn't know how to interpret.

"You know I would gladly kick some terrorist butt, if I needed to."

"That's what I'm afraid of." He turned and left the barn.

She watched him go, then led the horse into his stall, released him, stepped out and closed the gate. Hanging his lead rope and halter on the hook next to the door, she headed outside to inconspicuously clean up the tack around the hot-walker, well within earshot of the stud barn.

Rahul already had the horse unloaded and in the barn by the time Mac stepped around the nose of the truck and approached the entrance to the stable.

The intimidating sentries were no longer posted at the doorway. They'd disappeared the day Mac and Emma had removed Navigator from the stud barn, which seemed to indicate they'd only been there to keep an eye on him.

He slowed his pace, angling his head slightly to the right just in case he happened to catch a word of conversation going on inside the barn, but broken strings of Arabic were all he could make out as he darkened the doorway.

What he wouldn't do to be able to understand what they were saying. Maybe that was what got Victor killed? Maybe he'd figured out what was going down on Christmas Eve.

Caution mixed with confidence as he walked down the breezeway, keeping his focus on Rahul as he stood at the door of Dragon's stall, chattering to someone inside.

Rahul glanced up, his stare locking on him.

Mac raised his hand and pinned a friendly grin on his face as he moved in where he could see the action transpiring.

"Rahul. I trust you had a good trip?"

"Yes. Everything went smoothly."

Mac eyed the crime in progress, with Javas and Karif trying to bridle Dragon in the corner of the cubicle. The black colt was having none of it. Instead, he continued to strike out at them with his front hooves every time they got close.

"He is too much trouble. I plan to encourage my employer to sell him, or have him destroyed."

"After he runs in the Holiday Classic?" Mac asked.

"Yes, of course."

"Mind if I try?"

Rahul gestured with his hand while he rattled off a couple lines in Arabic to the men, fighting the horse as if he was a dragon.

Mac stepped into the stall. His senses went on alert and a measure of warning combed through him.

Was this how they'd suckered Victor in so they could kill him?

Javas and Karif stared at him as if he'd lost his mind, then handed him the headstall with a D-ring bit on it and shuffled out of the cubicle.

The sound of the stall door moving on its rollers made him nervous, but he didn't flinch. Were they hoping the unruly colt would smack him down so they could finish the job?

Mac raised his hand out in front of him like he'd seen his

father do. With calm, easy motions he reassured the frightened colt, watching his heavy breathing, rapid eye movements and head shy behavior begin to wane.

Somewhere in the stable he heard the familiar beat of counting in Arabic.

"Tiss-ah...sub-ah...wa-Had...ar-bah...ar-bah...kham-sah."

Dragon's Soul dropped his head low and shuffled toward Mac, a sure sign that he'd capitulated.

Mac stroked the colt's sweat-slicked coat, hearing the sound of Emma's voice outside in the corridor.

"Mac! Mac!"

The stall door slid open and he saw panic on her face.

His heart rate shot up. "What's going on?"

"It's Navigator, he's down in his stall."

He gave Dragon's Soul a final pat and lunged through the doorway, handing a stony-faced Rahul the bridle on the way out and falling in behind Emma, who was running along the breezeway.

Looking sideways he saw the other two grooms, Omar and Siraj, coming out of the cubicle that housed the new horse Rahul had just brought in. One of them had a notepad in his hand. More numbers.

They raced across the open paddock and ducked into the main barn, where Emma stopped and Mac continued. He'd seen the colt's future flash before his eyes in the time it took them to reach the barn.

He hurried to the stall, opened the latch and stepped inside, staring at the horse, who stood in the front corner eating from his feed bucket. He pulled his head out, eyeballed Mac for a moment and went back to his sweet feed.

"Emma. What the hell—"

"Shh." She glanced over at the barn door and stepped

inside the cubicle. "Keep your voice down, they might be listening."

He saw fear turn her body rigid.

Stepping closer, he whispered, "Tell me what's going on."

"I saw Karif and Javas hurry out of the stud barn a couple of minutes ago to get a tire iron out of the back of the pickup. They were heading back inside with it when I started yelling for you."

He took her into his arms, feeling her body shiver uncontrollably.

"They were going to use it to kill you, Mac, just like they murdered Victor."

And he'd fallen for it, dammit. If he hadn't calmed the colt, and Emma hadn't been paying attention...playing backup, he'd be history right now.

He held her until she stopped shaking.

Chapter Sixteen

Emma moved forward in line at the registration window with Navigator's paperwork in hand and her heart in her throat.

The buzz of excitement ignited the air in the room and gave her goose bumps.

Glancing around, she spotted Mac standing next to the entrance trying to look relaxed, but he couldn't fool her, not anymore.

Smiling at several of the owners she knew from competing farms, she waited patiently until it was her turn. She spotted Rahul two lines over, already at the window and handing over the paperwork to enter Dragon's Soul in the Holiday Classic.

Pulling in a breath, she averted her gaze and focused on the back of the man standing in front of her to keep from making eye contact with Rahul.

Since she'd managed to foil their attempt at smashing Mac's head in with a tire iron, she'd done everything she could to avoid coming in contact with Rahul and his crew, because she couldn't keep her obvious hatred from showing. Mac had run interference for her more than once in the last couple of days.

"Miss Clareborn," Rahul said, cutting the line to stand next to her. "Good luck running Navigator's Whim, I'm certain he can win."

"Thank you, Rahul. Good luck to Dragon's Soul."

Rahul nodded and smiled, but his cold black eyes belied the friendly gesture and once he left her side, she let her guard down and sucked in a deep breath. She would be glad when this was over and he was rotting in prison.

The man in front of her completed his entry transaction and left the window.

She stepped up and put her paperwork down.

"Firehill Farms, Old Lemons Road, Lexington, Kentucky." The woman examined the entry form, Doc Remington's vet report, her owner/trainer's license, her liability insurance card and the workman's comp paperwork. "Your check, Miss Clareborn."

Emma reached into her coat pocket and took out her personal check for the entry fee, squeezed it in her palm and put it down on the counter.

"Thank you. It looks like you have everything in order. I'll get your paperwork processed and give you a barn assignment, gate pass and a slot number in the paddock. Your pre-post time is three o'clock. Your horse will get one parade lap with a ponied-up track Steward who will lead him out of the paddock once your jockey is on board. From there you head to your owner-reserved box seat."

The woman sucked in a short breath and continued. "Your horse must load into the starting gate at precisely three-twenty, or he risks disqualification and you will forfeit your twenty-five-thousand-dollar entry fee."

Emma's stomach clenched with excitement. It was becoming so real she could almost taste it.

The race secretary pulled out her computer keyboard and began tapping in the information.

"How's it going?" Mac whispered against her ear.

She closed her eyes for an instant, then opened them again,

feeling more in charge of her emotions with him standing beside her. "You saw Rahul?"

"Yes."

"He wished us good luck. He says the colt could win."

"Did he."

The woman turned to her printer and began pulling out page after page.

Emma fidgeted, praying she could keep it all straight. Her father had always handled this stuff in the past, never her, but it was time she learned to manage things.

"Relax." Mac stroked his hand across her back. "I'll help you learn the paper routine. You've already done the hard stuff. You've raised and trained a winner, this is just your ticket to the gravy."

She leaned into him and he put his arm around her waist.

"You're all set, Miss Clareborn. Here's your race-day packet." She slid a thick manila envelope across the counter. "Have a nice day and good luck at the Holiday Classic."

Emma took the packet, put it in the purse she had slung across her body and stepped back.

"Excuse me." Mac leaned on the counter. "Can you tell me what barn Dragon's Soul will be in?"

"Certainly." The secretary tapped her keyboard and stared at the monitor on her right. "Barn five, stall twenty."

"Thank you." Mac turned around and followed Emma away from the window. They waded through the crowd of Thoroughbred owners swapping fastest times and horse tales and out into the parking lot.

Reaching out, he took Emma's elbow and pulled her to a stop. He scanned the lot. Rahul had beaten them out of the building by a few minutes, but somehow Mac couldn't shake the feeling he was still there, somewhere, watching, waiting.

"We did it, Mac. We really did it."

He took her hand and they headed for the pickup. He didn't relax until he had her safely inside on the seat next to him.

"It's a relief to have that over with. Now we just need to win."

"The colt has it covered, trust me." He fired up the truck and pulled out of the parking space, glancing in his rearview mirror as he circled the row of flashy cars lined up like a who's who of the best blue bloods in the bluegrass.

"I need a Derby hat for the race, Mac. Can we drive into Lexington to Ladies-and-Gents Hatters in Victorian Square?"

"Sure." He took a left out onto Iron Works Road from the parking lot and watched a sleek black car pull out one car behind them.

"That's on Main, right?"

"Yes."

He remembered the quaint mall that had been around since before he was born. He was pretty sure the hatters was where his dad had purchased the fedora he liked to wear now.

Relief glided over his nerves as he glanced up and saw the black car turn then disappear down a side street.

Sucking in some of the excitement he could feel in the air, he headed for Victorian Square. He had some Christmas shopping of his own to take care of.

MAC FIRST NOTICED the car's headlights in his rearview mirror as he headed out of New Zion and turned onto Lemons Mill Pike.

The vehicle came up fast behind him, swung out and whipped around them at a high rate of speed.

He recognized the black car that had followed them out of the parking lot at Keeneland and felt the first wave of warning ripple across his mind.

"Damn, that guy's driving too fast for this stretch of road."

Emma watched the taillights fade to tiny red pinpricks in the darkness.

"That car followed us out of the lot at the horse park this afternoon and into Lexington, but he turned off on a side street. I wasn't sure if it was intentional or coincidence."

"I guess you're getting your answer. So what's he doing out here now?" She watched the car's brake lights come on in the distance.

"You buckled up?" Mac asked.

"Always." Worry ground over her nerves. She didn't like the sound of that. Was he anticipating some sort of trouble? She'd had enough of it to last her a lifetime. She was ready for it to stop.

The red lights vanished and her nerves calmed, only to tighten again when headlights on bright shined up ahead in the darkness.

"Looks like he's coming back at us," Mac said, staring straight ahead.

Fear rocked Emma's senses. She couldn't seem to swallow the lump caught just below her windpipe. Mentally she drove the road ahead for hazards and felt her body tense.

"The bridge over North Elkhorn Creek is between us and him."

Mac eyeballed the speedometer, slowed down and dialed up the spot she was talking about in his mind's eye.

The stream was wide there, the bridge span sixty feet across, the deep, slow-moving water ten feet below.

A game of chicken? Mac knew his truck easily outweighed the sleek car and a meeting on the bridge would be suicide.

His headlights illuminated the narrow reflective panels on either side of the concrete abutment a hundred yards ahead. He had no intention of sharing any part of the bridge with the oncoming car.

Mac slammed on the brakes.

An explosion went off, like a firecracker igniting in a can.

A tire blew.

The truck jerked hard to the left.

Smoke belched from the left front wheel well and streamed past the driver's side window.

Mac fought to control the slide, but the pickup careened across the center line.

Emma screamed.

Resigned to the situation, he worked to mitigate the impact and steered into the skid, but it was already too late.

The edge of the road was there before he could right the momentum.

Mac heard the front wheels rip through the gravel on the shoulder as the truck flipped over and rolled down the steep embankment.

The air bags inside the cab deployed.

He counted the revolutions. Once, twice and the final bone-jarring impact as the still-running pickup slammed down on its top.

Mac got his bearings in the mayhem.

He was hanging upside down, still wearing his seat belt. He stared out the shattered front windshield at a single beam of light shining from one headlight. They'd landed inches from the water.

The last-minute maneuver had saved them from a hard plunge into Elkhorn Creek and certain death.

"Emma?" He reached up, found the seat-belt buckle and released it.

Dropping like a rock, he crumpled against the roof, now a floor, unfolded and eased forward on his knees.

"Can you hear me, Em?" Desperation fisted in his chest. He reached across in the direction of the passenger seat, feeling her hair brush his hand.

"Emma!" Straining, he found her buckle clasp and released her, pulling her into his arms as she dropped out of the restraint.

She was unconscious but alive.

The wail of an engine being revved blended with the sound of the still-idling pickup.

Another problem emerged on the air inside of the crushed cab, its caustic vapors setting off warning bells inside his head as he breathed them in.

Gasoline.

It must be leaking out of the fuel-tank valve on the right side of the upside-down pickup.

He had to get Emma out of the truck.

Now.

Mac pushed backward with one arm locked around Emma's waist and the other balanced on the floor. He aimed for the driver's side window, shuffling over broken glass that cut into his knees, shins and hands. He ignored the sting and kept moving.

He found the opening with one boot-clad foot and determined the glass was missing. With his heel, he kicked loose what remained of the window.

First one foot, then the other. He went to his belly, dragging Emma along half a foot at a time and praying the opening was large enough for him to squeeze his upper body out of.

If it wasn't...

Semiconscious, Emma felt the sensation of being pulled along. The feel of Mac's strong arm wrapped around her midsection seemed to be her only connection to a disassembled reality she fought to clarify.

Crash. They'd been in a car crash. She remembered the tinny ring of an explosion right before Mac lost control of the truck and they went over the edge just shy of the bridge.

Down, he was pulling her down. Taking his arm away from around her waist. Was he leaving?

Terror roared to the forefront and she jolted into the conscious world, feeling the sharp prick of glass cutting into her backside.

Sucking in a ragged breath, she opened her eyes, staring at the eerie reflection of light on the bucket seats above her head. They were upside down.

In a panic, she attempted to roll over, but the space was too small.

"Mac! I can't breathe."

"Hang on, Em, I'm going to pull you out through the window, but you need to raise your arms over your head."

She did as he asked and felt him grasp her wrists. Bending her knees, she pushed off the instant he pulled and held her breath through the tight squeeze as he wedged her out of the narrow opening onto the ground next to him.

"Keep your head down; they're sitting up on the road." Panic dissolved her composure and Mac reached out and cupped his hand over her mouth. "It's best to let them believe we didn't make it."

She nodded.

He pulled his hand away, but she'd already made so much noise they had to know they were still alive.

Ping! A gunshot rang out from the road above. A bullet drilled into the underside of the pickup.

Mac's nerves turned on edge, his mind shifting into overdrive. He unholstered his weapon and took Emma's hand. "There's gasoline leaking out on the other side of the truck. If they hit it they'll spark a fireball. We've got to get clear."

She squeezed his fingers so hard they burned.

Mac stared off into the overgrown field they'd rolled into, spotting a cluster of brush twenty-five feet out from where they huddled. If they could take cover there, they had a chance.

Ping! Another shot ripped into the pickup.

"Can you run?" He stared into the shadow of her face in the gloom.

"Yeah. I feel a little loopy. I hit my head, but my legs work."

"Do you see that patch of brush over there?" He pointed it out, glad when she focused on it. "That's where we're going when I return fire. Twenty-five feet, sweetheart. Just twenty-five feet."

She nodded.

Mac aimed high and over his left shoulder and squeezed off a round.

Someone returned fire from the road.

"Go, Emma. Run!"

She took off.

Mac fell in behind her, getting off a round a second as he worked to cover her body with his own.

They reached the brush and dived into it.

Mac stared out, took aim and pulled the trigger, hitting the left rear quarter panel of the car.

The thug squeezed off two more rounds. His bullet hit the pickup just below the leaking gas tank and ignited the vapors.

Woof! The truck's gas tank exploded in a raging ball of fire that lit up the night sky.

In the glare and heat Mac saw a single individual standing on the road next to the black car, but he didn't recognize him.

He jumped in and sped away.

"Mac, your truck!" He pulled Emma against him and planted a kiss on the top of her head. "It's replaceable. I'll get a new one." Digging in his coat pocket, he took out his cell phone, dialed 911 and requested an ambulance, fire truck and Sheriff Riley Wilkes.

He shut the phone and held on to her, watching the flames destroy the hunk of metal, and appreciated how close he'd just come to losing her.

The woman in his arms was irreplaceable.

Closing his eyes he acknowledged the revelation that was locked up inside of him.

He was in love with her, too.

EMMA SAT ON THE BACK bumper of the ambulance staring at Mac and Sheriff Wilkes as they talked just out of earshot.

The commotion clouded the scene, and she found herself shutting it all out as she watched him. Her ears were still ringing from the noise of the explosion.

"Look at the light for me, miss," an EMT said, focusing a penlight first in one eye, then in the other. "Her pupils are equal and reactive. She's oriented and alert."

"I'd like to go home now. My farm is only a couple of miles from here."

"You took a bump on the head. You've got a minor concussion."

"I know the drill. I promise I'll take care of myself and call the doctor if I have any problems."

One EMT handed the other one a clipboard. "Sign this. It's a release form stating that you don't want to be transported to the hospital."

She took the clipboard and the pen and signed at the X, then handed it back and stood up. "Thank you."

Turning, she headed for Mac and the sheriff.

"This was no accident. Whoever was driving that car set off a charge that took out my left front tire. They wanted us to crash into the creek."

"Did you get a look at the plate number?"

"No, but I'm pretty sure it was a black Lexus."

Emma reached Mac's side and huddled next to him, feeling the nip of the cold for the first time tonight.

"I'll put a bulletin out on the car, but there are dozens that fit that description cruising the streets of Lexington this close to race day."

"I know I hit it at least once in the rear quarter panel. A nice car like that with a bullet hole in it will turn up somewhere to be repaired."

Wilkes nodded, and Mac reached out and put his arm around Emma. "Can we catch a ride home, Sheriff?"

"Sure, hop in."

They fell in behind Wilkes as he headed for his patrol car.

Home.

He liked the sound of that and the sure feel of Emma next to him. What he didn't like was his fear that Rahul had brought another crew member on board who had no qualms about trying to kill them.

Chapter Seventeen

Mac closed the gate on the back of the horse trailer and went around to the driver's side door of Firehill's bright red truck. Leaning against it, he waited for Emma to come out of the house so they could leave for Keeneland.

Tension knotted his muscles and sucked all the excitement out of the air. Glancing over, he watched Rahul and Karif working to load Dragon's Soul into their horse trailer. He gritted his teeth.

It had been three days since the accident on Lemons Mill Pike and he'd been on full alert since the black Lexus with his bullet hole in it had turned up in a ditch a mile from where they'd crashed. It had been reported stolen by an elderly couple in Lexington the day of the entry sign-up. Another dead end.

Today it would all be over, at least, that's what Agent Donahue had said in the early hours before dawn, when they'd wired Mac for sound with a hidden microphone and laid out their plan to let things unfold so they could crush the cell.

The screen door at the back of the house banged shut.

Mac straightened and eyed Emma as she walked toward him in a dressy chocolate-colored pants suit, and wearing her cowboy boots. "Hey, gorgeous."

She looked up and gave him a tired smile. She'd been getting about as much sleep as he had with a pack of trouble living next door.

"It's finally here. Race day." Emma tried to relax, but she couldn't. She knew if she turned around she'd see Rahul and his crew. That was the last thing she needed right now. "Can we go?"

"Yeah." Mac followed her around to the passenger-side door and pulled it open for her. She climbed in. He closed it and came back around, got into the truck and fired it up. "Where's your dad?"

"He told me to go, said he's going to watch the race on the tube."

He shifted the truck into gear and eased down on the gas pedal.

Emma put on her seat belt and clutched the race packet in her hand. They'd be at Keeneland in less than half an hour and she started to count the minutes as they pulled out of the farm onto the main road.

MAC HANDED THE GATE PASS to the uniformed security guard at the entrance into barn row.

He looked it over, handed it back, then waved them through the wide gate and into the long line of horsemen jockeying for parking to unload their horses.

Taking a right turn, he headed for their assigned barn, spotting barn number seven, one stable from the end of the row. He found a pull-through relatively close, eased the truck and trailer in and stopped. "We made it."

"Beats the heck out of the alternative." She looked over at him and he reached out to touch her hand as she slid it across the seat toward him.

"Agent Donahue has the place surrounded." He interlocked his fingers with hers.

"How do you know that?"

"He told me this morning."

She looked away and blinked back tears then straightened. "Does he have any idea what they're going to try?"

"No." If reassurance was his mark he failed to hit it. "Just keep your eyes open, Emma. Let me know if you see anything suspicious."

"I can do that." She reached for the door handle and climbed out of the truck.

Mac followed, hearing the nervous colt whinny in the back of the trailer. "Let's check out his stall first, then I'll unload him. Barn seven, stall twenty-one, right there on the end."

Together they found the cubicle bedded with fresh straw. Mac opened the stable door and went inside, turned on the water valve and filled the trough half-full. "Looks ready. I'll go get the colt."

Emma waited next to the stable gate, watching Mac enter the slant trailer and lead Navigator's Whim out.

The colt was excited. He shuffled sideways and let out a high-pitched whinny, drawing responses from all over the horse park.

She could feel it, too. The early afternoon air was heavy with excitement, some of which rubbed off on her and infused the race grounds with an energy level that was off the charts.

Sunshine glistened across Navigator's shiny red-brown coat, highlighting the colt's impressive athleticism. Her heart fluttered in her chest. He was going to win today. Her elation waned slightly when she spotted Rahul and Karif pulling in to a space not too far from where Mac had parked Firehill's rig.

They climbed out of the truck and begin unloading Dragon's Soul. The big black horse bolted out of the trailer and they fought to get him under control, which always seemed to be a challenge.

She had to look away, had to refocus on something she could control or her nerves would fray. They had two hours to get the colt ready before he went to the paddock. She would start there.

MAC STUDIED THE HORSEMEN milling in the paddock from his spot in post slot box number five, looking for trouble and hoping he'd see it in time to stop it.

On the other side of the narrow paddock, Rahul and Karif worked to control Dragon's Soul. Turning and heading him into post slot number thirteen for the fourth time.

Mac got the sense that the animal disliked them as much as they seemed to dislike him. The colt had good instincts.

"Grady should be here any minute now." Emma checked her watch for the umpteenth time before making sure the thin blanket bearing the colt's name and his number, five, was evenly spaced under the flat saddle. "He's ready."

"Relax, Emma," Mac said in a tone that reassured her she'd done everything she could to prepare the horse, and then some.

She fidgeted and looked at him, trying to absorb a fraction of his calm, even though her stomach was doing flip-flops. She glanced away, her gaze falling on box slot thirteen. "Look over there, Mac. I think Abadar just showed up."

The hair on the back of Mac's neck bristled. Would Abadar recognize him? He reached into his shirt pocket, pulled out his sunglasses and slipped them on. Agent Donahue had coached him and Emma on how to handle the meeting. Recognition could cause a whole series of problems, even alert the terrorists to his association with the sheikh.

Tension twisted the muscles between his shoulder blades as he stepped back into the box, watching discreetly when Rahul pointed in their direction. Abadar wore a traditional kandora robe and a kaffiyeh secured by a black ekal on his head. He turned, looked and headed in their direction.

"Greet him, Emma, that's all you have to do." Mac pivoted and began to rub his hands over the colt, double-checking the equipment with his back to the box opening.

"Miss Clareborn?"

Emma steeled herself and stared into the face of Sheikh Ahmed Abadar, into his narrowed black eyes, and wondered why on earth Mac had almost lost his life to save this man.

"Yes. You must be Sheikh Abadar. It's good to finally meet you."

"Rahul tells me you have given him notice to vacate Fire-hill. I hope we have not wronged you in any way."

She reran every warning Agent Donahue had given her about causing a scene, or drawing attention. "Consider your accounts paid until the day after tomorrow, when I expect that you will have all of your horses transported off of the farm."

"It is agreed. They will all be gone the day after to-morrow."

Mac moved around the horse, feeling the colt's legs. He closed his eyes for a moment, listening to the sound of Aba-dar's voice, but something about it wasn't right.

"Good luck in the race, Miss Clareborn. Your horse is impressive."

The voice was an octave higher and lacked the thick accent he'd listened to in the week he'd spent guarding the sheikh in Louisville prior to the shooting.

"Thank you. Good luck to you."

Mac raised up and turned around at the last second to get a good look at the man just before he turned away. He bore a striking resemblance to the sheikh, but he wasn't Ahmed Abadar, and he'd seen him before, the night of the crash.

He was the man from the black Lexus.

Easing out into the walkway, Mac caught a glimpse of a silver briefcase in Abadar's hand as it pressed into the folds of his kandora.

The imposter met Karif in the middle of the paddock as the field of jockeys filed out of their staging area, followed by a string of ponied-up stewards, ready to take the horses to post.

"That's not Ahmed." He repeated it again, but louder, and hoped like hell Agent Donahue was listening at the other end of the microphone. "He's not Sheikh Abadar, he's an imposter."

Emma glanced at him for a moment and met Grady in front of the box. "He's all yours." She unlatched the double leads on the colt and led him out of the box.

"Rider up." Mac caught Grady's boot and hoisted him onto Navigator's Whim.

A steward fell in beside horse and rider as they moved around the outside of the paddock, headed for the parade lap.

The air locked up in Mac's lungs as he witnessed Abadar hand the briefcase he was carrying over to Karif.

Briefcase?

Whatever they had planned involved the briefcase. That's what Victor had been trying to tell him the night he died.

"Mac, what's going on?" Emma reached out and clutched his forearm.

"Go to the box seat, Emma. Stay there. Promise me you'll stay there."

She felt the tension in his body, saw it in the rigid set of his jaw as he stared at her.

"I love you, Emma. I should have told you sooner." He leaned down and kissed her on the mouth, then walked away in a hurry.

Her throat closed. Fear welled in her veins as she watched

him weave through the horsemen in the paddock and disappear around the end of the boxes right behind Karif, who now carried the mysterious silver briefcase she'd seen the sheikh holding only moments before.

Where the hell was Donahue?

MAC HUNG AT THE BACK corner of the slot barn and watched Karif cross the open area and turn down the row between barns four and five.

He pushed away from cover and ran straight across to barn two. Karif had to be headed for Dragon's Soul's stall on the inside row of barn five.

Did he have a bomb? Some sort of biological weapon in the briefcase? Mac wasn't sure, he only knew that whatever they had planned was happening now.

"I hope to hell you're listening, Donahue," he said as he jogged the corridor between stable two and three. "It's happening now. Barn five, stall twenty."

A couple of grooms looked at him as if he was crazy as he hurried past them and pulled up at the end of the row. Poking his head out, he scanned the busy area between the clusters of stables, then hustled across to the end of barn four.

Mac unholstered his weapon. Keeping it low, he hung close to the far right corner, and leaned out, spotting the top of Karif's head just before he dropped behind the four-foot-tall wall panel of the stall.

Caution ignited in Mac's veins.

He pulled in a breath, stayed low and headed across the open space between the barns.

Reaching the corner, he went flat against the outside wall and turned to face it so he could listen for the sound of Karif's movements inside.

"Kham-sah…ith-nain…sit-ah…tiss-ah…ar-bah…ith-nain."

The hair on the back of Mac's neck bristled. It was the same familiar rhythm of counting he'd heard in Firehill's stud barn. The numbers they'd been writing down from the tattoos on the horses' upper lips.

"Thah-mahn-ee-ah…thah-lath-ah…sit-ah…sub-ah… wa-Had…ar-bah."

Mac eased his head around the corner and stared into the stall through a narrow crack at the edge where the panels joined.

Karif knelt next to the open briefcase with a notepad in his hand, reading off numbers in a series of six as he punched them into a digital timer inside the case.

Mac's blood turned cold.

"Bomb," he whispered into the hidden mic, praying Donahue showed up in the next minute, because it looked as if the numbers were about to run out.

Mac charged the stall gate and kicked it open.

It banged against the inside wall.

Karif pulled back and stared at him, then at the gun in his hand, then back up into his face.

"Get back!" he yelled, motioning with his head to the opposite corner of the stall.

Karif inched away from the briefcase.

Caution rocked Mac's nerves as he stared at Karif and watched his eyes narrow. "Get the hell in here, Donahue!" he shouted, holding a bead on Karif's chest with his finger on the trigger.

He heard a commotion on his right in the doorway of the stall, and expected to see Agent Donahue busting in with a string of armed agents. Instead he found himself staring into Emma's fearful brown eyes, then into Rahul's black ones as he pushed her through the open stall door in a chokehold.

"Karif. Continue with the detonation codes."

Mac turned the gun on Rahul and aimed for his forehead, prepared to blow his brains out, but Emma was too close.

Karif crawled back to the briefcase and began punching in numbers again.

Emma sucked in a breath and made her decision. She raised her right foot and jammed her boot into Rahul's shin.

He let out a yelp.

She drilled her elbow back into his ribs as hard as she could.

His arm on her throat went slack for an instant.

She dropped away from him, diving for the pitchfork leaning against the wall next to the gate.

Pop! Pop!

She heard the crack of Mac's gun and saw Karif drop into the straw next to the case.

Snagging the fork, she whirled around and pinned Rahul to the wooden gate with the tines through the shoulder of his jacket, inches from his neck.

"Go, go, go!" Agent Donahue yelled to his men as they rushed into the cubicle, guns drawn.

Mac holstered his weapon and pulled Emma into his arms, staring over her head at Agent Donahue and a bomb specialist who hurried into the stall and went to his knees next to the case. The color dropped from the man's face as he rocked back and stared up at Donahue.

"Son of a bitch. You just saved us from World War Three, Mr. Titus. This is a nuclear detonator, and somewhere within a hundred yards is a nuke." He reached out, took the crumpled notepad from Karif's lifeless hand and stared at it. "He only had two more numbers to enter in the detonation code sequence and it would have been over for all of us."

Emma's knees buckled. Mac held her up. "Could be in their horse trailer in the parking lot."

Agent Donahue nodded to one of his men, who left the stall

in search of the device. "I just learned ten minutes ago that the real Sheikh Ahmed Abadar's body was found in Bahrain a week ago, but he's been dead for over a month. Apparently he'd figured out the cell was planning to use his identity, his diplomatic immunity and his racehorse stable to plan some sort of attack on U.S. soil, and he was helping our government root them out."

That explained the high-level secret talks in Louisville that the sheikh had been engaged in with someone from the Pentagon, and why Mac had been forced to take a bullet to protect him. He'd do it again.

"You mean to tell me they piecemealed the components into the country one at a time, and smuggled the detonation codes in disguised as tattoos inside the horse's mouths out at Firehill?"

"Looks that way. We would have known exactly what they were up to if the codes had been verbalized on any one of the chatter sites we've been monitoring."

"What about the sheikh's horses?"

"Don't know if any of them are even his. So it looks like until we know differently, you've got nine additions to the Firehill stable." Agent Donahue grinned. "You're welcome to join the NSA, Mac. We could use someone like you in the organization."

"Thanks, but I've already got a job protecting Firehill Farm for a long time—that is, if the farmer's daughter will have me."

In the distance he heard the race bugle blowing the traditional notes of the call-to-post. "We've got a horse in that race, Donahue. We'll catch up with you later, give you our statements."

Donahue nodded. "I'll see you both after the Winner's Circle.

Mac took Emma's hand and hurried out of the stall.

THE CLAPPER VIBRATED between the iron bells and the starting gate sprung open. "And they're off," the announcer shouted over the PA system.

Emma stood next to Mac at the rail, watching Navigator's Whim break from the number-five gate and thunder into the middle of the pack, gravitating toward the inside rail.

She wasn't sure if it was the horse race, the man standing next to her who'd said he loved her or the fact that they'd stopped an attack that would have wiped out the entire blue-grass region. Any way she figured it, her heart was racing, too.

Mac squeezed her fingers and moved her down the rail, aiming for the finish line. His eyes fixed on Dragon's Soul as he took last position in the field of fifteen horses.

"Come on, Dragon," he coaxed, watching the shiny black colt move up a length.

"Polly's Day crosses the line. Joker's Rule in second, and Texas Two Step a length back in third place as they move into the first turn."

Mac looked up and spotted an opening on the first level. They hurried for it; he needed elevation to see the backstretch. They climbed the stairs and turned to watch the race.

"Polly's Day fades to third as the pack moves into the clubhouse turn. Joker's Rule is in first, and here comes Dragon's Soul on the outside, with Navigator's Whim a length ahead."

Mac held his breath, watching both of the colts meet up at the head of the pack. Time slowed.

Emma squeezed him arm. "Come on, Navigator, come on, babe, you can do it."

"The pack is fading, folks. It's number five Navigator's Whim moving to the inside on the rail as they power down the homestretch. Number thirteen Dragon's Soul in second,

Joker's Rule two lengths back in third. Vagabond is fourth. Dixie Driver is in fifth."

He focused on the wire, watching the colts change up gears at the same instant.

Neck and neck they reached for the finish line, then Navigator pulled ahead of Dragon's Soul by a length and surged under the wire.

"And it's number five Navigator's Whim with the win! Dragon's Soul comes across the line in second and Joker's Rule takes third. Followed by Vagabond in fourth, and Dixie Driver in the money in fifth place."

Mac pulled Emma into his arms and lowered his mouth to hers, feeling the rush of need overwhelm his system as he kissed her like a starving man.

He pulled back and stared down into her face. "I love you, Em."

Emma's heart squeezed in her chest. She went up onto her tiptoes and kissed Mac again for good measure.

"I have a Thoroughbred farm, you know, and I need a bodyguard around to make sure it's always safe. Can I interest you in a lifetime position?" She smiled up at him and felt her cheeks heat.

"I thought you'd never ask." He took her hand and they headed for the Winner's Circle.

MAC HELD THE TWO STEAMING cups of mint cocoa and waited for Emma to settle in the porch swing. He handed her a mug and took his place beside her.

"Can you believe it? This whole time, my dad's nurse, Samantha, has been helping him learn to walk again so he could surprise me on Christmas Eve. He says he'll be jogging before the Kentucky Derby rolls around in May, and he wants to sit in the owner's box before he walks to the Winner's Circle."

He reached out and smoothed a strand of hair behind her

ear, watching her eyes close for an instant, then open as she turned to look at him in the twinkle of the tree lights shining through the window.

"It was good to see him get up out of his wheelchair, Em, and walk down the hall. He's going to do it. He's going to make it." Mac put his mug on the porch rail behind him, took hers from her hand and set it on the railing, as well. He'd saved the best of Christmas Eve for now. "We all made it. We survived this day, and that's a miracle all by itself."

"I'm just glad it's over. I need normal in my life." Emma stared at Mac, at the quirky smile on his mouth and a glimmer in his eyes she'd never seen before. "I have something for you."

"Really? I've got something for you, too."

She shivered, hoping it involved the entirety of the night, a warm bed and his body next to hers.

Reaching inside her coat, she pulled out a rolled-up piece of paper tied with a strand of red ribbon. "This is long overdue, Mac. Merry Christmas."

Mac reached out and took the gift from her, but there was really only one thing he wanted. He watched her eyes widen with excitement and a smile broaden on her lips as he pulled the ribbon loose and unscrolled the page.

He read through the legalities and felt the air lock in his lungs.

"We talked about it and made the decision last week. My father always intended to give Paul back his share of Smooth Sailing when he sobered up, but he never came back. So as his son, you have a right to what belonged to him."

Mac's throat tightened. "I don't know what to say. A half share in Navigator's Whim is too much, Em. I can't take—" She leaned in and kissed him, shutting the protest inside of him forever. He kissed her back and pulled her into his arms.

His heart expanded inside his chest and he broke the kiss, reached into his coat pocket and pulled out his gift to her.

"Then let's at least keep him in the family." He opened the ring box and watched her tear up. "I want you always, Emma Clareborn. Will you have me?"

"I thought you'd never ask."

For Immediate Release to the Press
Kentucky Derby–Churchill Downs
Louisville, Kentucky

Mr. and Mrs. Mac Calliway Titus and Mr. Thadeous Clareborn, all of Firehill Farm in Lexington, stood proudly in the Winner's Circle on Saturday with their horse Navigator's Whim, blanketed in Kentucky Derby roses. The cream of the story rests with the second-place finisher, Dragon's Soul, a horse that also hails from Firehill Farm. The heated rivalry between the two magnificent colts is sure to go down in horse-racing history as the battle of the decade. It was a breathtaking race in the homestretch, but Navigator's Whim pulled it out by a length. Stay tuned, because Firehill plans to take this colt all the way to the Triple Crown.

* * * * *

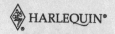 HARLEQUIN®

INTRIGUE®

COMING NEXT MONTH

Available November 9, 2010

#1239 BODY ARMOR
Bodyguard of the Month
Alana Matthews

#1240 HIGH-CALIBER CHRISTMAS
Whitehorse, Montana: Winchester Ranch Reloaded
B.J. Daniels

#1241 COLBY BRASS
Colby Agency: Christmas Miracles
Debra Webb

#1242 SAVIOR IN THE SADDLE
Texas Maternity: Labor and Delivery
Delores Fossen

#1243 THE PEDIATRICIAN'S PERSONAL PROTECTOR
The Delancey Dynasty
Mallory Kane

#1244 HOSTAGE TO THUNDER HORSE
Elle James

LARGER-PRINT BOOKS!

GET 2 FREE LARGER-PRINT NOVELS
PLUS 2 FREE GIFTS!

HILP10R

HARLEQUIN®

A *Romance*

FOR EVERY MOOD™

Spotlight on

Inspirational

Wholesome romances
that touch the heart and soul.

See the next page
to enjoy a sneak peek from
the Love Inspired® Suspense
inspirational series.

*See below for a sneak peek from
our inspirational line, Love Inspired® Suspense*

*Enjoy this heart-stopping excerpt from
RUNNING BLIND
by top author Shirlee McCoy,
available November 2010!*

*The mission trip to Mexico was supposed to be an
adventure. But the thrill turns sour when Jenna Dougherty
and her roommate Magdalena are kidnapped.*

"It's okay. I'm here to help." The voice was as deep as the
darkness, but Jenna Dougherty didn't believe the lie. She
could do nothing but lie still as hands slid down her arms,
felt the rope around her wrists.

"I'm going to use a knife to cut you free, Jenna. Hold
still."

The cold blade of a knife pressed close to her head before
her gag fell away.

"I—" she started, but her mouth was dry, and she could
do nothing but suck in air.

"Shhh. Whatever needs to be said can be said when
we're out of here." Nick spoke quietly, his hand gentle on
her cheek. There and gone as he sliced through the ropes on
her wrists and ankles.

He pulled her upright. "Come on. We may be on
borrowed time."

"I can't leave my friend," Jenna rasped out.

"There's no one here. Just us."

"She has to be here." Jenna took a step away.

"There's no one here. Let's go before that changes."

"It's dark. Maybe if we find a light…"

"What did you say?"

"We need to turn on the light. I can't leave until I know that—"

"What can you see, Jenna?"

"Nothing."

"No shadows? No light?"

"No."

"It's broad daylight. There's light spilling in from the window I climbed in through. You can't see it?"

She went cold at his words.

"I can't see anything."

"You've got a nasty bruise on your forehead. Maybe that has something to do with it." His fingers traced the tender flesh on her forehead.

"It doesn't matter *how* it happened. I'm blind!"

Can Nick help Jenna find her friend or will chasing this trail have Jenna running blindly again into danger?

Find out in RUNNING BLIND, available in November 2010 only from Love Inspired Suspense.